Three *Kisses* More

Jade Church

Three Kisses More by Jade Church First published in Great Britain by Jade Church in 2022

Paperback ISBN 978-1-7391457-7-4

Ebook ISBN 978-1-7391457-6-7

Also by Jade Church

Temper the Flame

This Never Happened

Get Even (Sun City #1)

In Too Deep (Living in Cincy #1)

Coming soon:

Fall Hard (Sun City #2)

Tempt My Heart (Living in Cincy #2)

The Clarity of Light (Kingdom of Stars #2)

Content Warning

Three Kisses More contains themes and content that some readers may find triggering, this includes but is not limited to: *brief mentions of fatphobia, slut shaming and misogyny, alcohol, blood (brief mention), death of a parent (brief mention, off page), cheating (past, ex, off page)*. Please note, this book also contains on-page sex, swearing, and nudity.

Three *Kisses* More

Jade Church

CHAPTER 1
Sephy

The worst part about travelling over the holidays was the airport. It was always filled with screaming kids and frazzled parents and even more tired staff. It was the time of the year that plenty of people dreaded, including me. The holidays, specifically Christmas for my family, were hell.

I was an introvert and truthfully my parents were exhausting at the best of times, but then with the addition of my brother and my cousins and my grandparents on my dad's side and – well, to say I was *happy* to be going on this three-week conference was an understatement.

Even if I did have to give a small speech at the end of the trip.

Having to work over Christmas would probably be considered most people's nightmare. And while, of course, there'd be no actual work happening on Christmas Day and Boxing Day itself, I found myself grateful for the reprieve. It was a big deal that I'd been asked to come on this trip and even more exciting that I'd been tapped for the closing speech – for a while I hadn't been sure that staying at the firm had been the right decision, but everything was starting to pay-off. *Quinnings* was a big league banking company and they'd clearly done well this year to be inviting so many of us on this work retreat. Last year it had been for the directors only, a pretence of work while they all skied no doubt.

I'd made it through security and all the way up to my gate with plenty of time and it was a good thing I'd left so early or that might not have been the case. I'd dodged not one but *two* instances of sticky fingers as a stray child escaped a harried looking parent and ran almost directly at me. *Then* I'd nearly joined the queue for the Wetherspoons by accident, mistaking it for the toilet line.

My department had paid for speedy boarding and I was in first class too, which would be a new experience. To be honest, it felt like the least they could do after how hard my team and I had been working the past few months. The majority of people had flown out yesterday but I'd had a few last-minute things to tie up at the office and had opted to fly out early today so I could finish up. I couldn't say I was sorry to miss the group flight. I liked my team, they were great, but I'd prefer to stick my headphones on and nap rather than make small talk.

It was an early flight, but I was kind of hoping

they'd still offer us booze. I probably should have been feeling a little guilty about missing the big family Christmas get-together, but all I could manage was relief. My brother, Jay, was only a few years older than me but we were polar opposites. He had a big personality and generally wasn't shy about keeping it under wraps. I loved him, but he could be exhausting and after everything that had happened the past year… I was long overdue for a break.

I'd stowed my overhead bags with little fuss and was pleased to find my seat was next to the window. I hardly ever got to fly anywhere, usually my holidays stayed within the U.K. or I took the train abroad because it was sometimes cheaper. We took off with a jolt that alarmed me for a second and my ears popped as we climbed into the sky. The flight attendant passed around complimentary breakfast and I grinned down at the cheap prosecco that came with my croissant and fruit salad. It would probably taste like crap, but it was *free*. *Happy fucking Christmas to me,* I thought as I took a sip and winced. The guy one seat over from me grinned as he took a taste of his.

"Five o'clock somewhere, huh."

I laughed politely and then looked away, just glad to finally be in the air as I reached for my headphones. The ski resort *Quinnings* had booked was apparently super fancy and while I wouldn't be on the slopes at any point, I was excited to try out the sauna. I'd never been in one before and had packed both a bikini and an all-in-one, unsure what was deemed 'appropriate' for sweating with strangers. A faint blush tickled my cheeks and I willed it away. Maybe there was one person I wouldn't mind sweating with a little more than the others.

Of course, it was a terrible idea and he wasn't anything more than an occasionally flirtatious friend, though maybe I was reading into his small comments more than they warranted. It didn't help that he was technically my boss… and the Big Boss' son. But what harm was there in fantasising? It wasn't like anything would happen. Probably.

"Visiting family for the holidays?" The guy in the aisle seat asked and I turned back to him with a smile that froze when I met his eyes. Holy hell.

"Er," I said inelegantly and gulped some more of my cheap prosecco as I paused my music. "No, actually. I'm on a business trip."

A dark eyebrow raised. "Me too. You're not out here with *Quinnings* are you?"

Great. Small talk after all. I was surprised anyone else had opted for this early morning flight instead of the more sleep-friendly one that had been available yesterday. I was even more taken aback by the fact that this guy was American, though I was pretty sure that we had people coming from a variety of our offices abroad but I wasn't sure why he'd bother coming to the UK first unless he wanted to check out our London office. Seemed a long way to travel to look at boring grey cubicles and a glass lift.

"Oh! I am, actually."

"Cool," he said with a slight smile and I stared for a second longer than was necessary.

"Cool."

We lapsed back into silence and after a moment I pulled my eyes away from his face and stared resolutely back out of the window as I hit play on *Dua Lipa*. What was I doing? This was ridiculous, I'd dated a little since Seth and I had broken up a year or so ago, but nobody serious. Not that this random attractive stranger had the potential to be someone serious. Or even someone at all.

I wanted to groan but bit it back so I didn't seem even weirder. My brain had the tendency to overthink things a little. I had what my parents always called an overactive imagination.

I was so lost in my own thoughts that I almost missed it when he tried to talk to me again.

"Pretty brutal of them getting us out here over Christmas, right?" His American accent was so thick that I found myself fascinated by the way his mouth shaped his vowels – *Quinnings* was an international company but other than the occasional video meeting I'd not had the chance to interact with anyone from our other offices yet. Really, I didn't even know everyone in our London office, let alone abroad, but it was true that I didn't really go out of my way to make new friends either. Talking to new people… well, it was something I was working on.

"Oh I'm actually happy to be here. It's always a nightmare at my parent's every year around the holidays." I bit my lip, realising I probably sounded all *bah humbug* and was relieved when he laughed.

"Fuck, I'm so glad it's not just me. Plus, I heard the Christmas Eve parties are always great."

"There's free drinks," I offered and he grinned, his teeth white and even except for his bottom canine which was a little crooked. It was cute.

No. Not cute! It was a tooth! Teeth weren't cute.

"So are you new to the company then?" He seemed surprised and I smiled. "If you haven't been to one of the Christmas parties," I explained.

"Yes actually, I only signed my contract last week."

"Oh wow, welcome I guess!"

He chuckled as we clunked our plastic prosecco glasses together. "Thanks." We sipped quietly before he looked back up at me and smiled, his brown eyes warm and friendly. "I'm Drew, by the way."

"Sephy," I said and shook the hand he was holding out, surprised when he lifted it to his mouth and pressed a quick but firm kiss to its back that sent a line of heat through my chest.

The *bing-bong* of an aircraft announcement made Drew look up in time to miss the blush skating its way across my cheeks.

"Good morning this is your Captain speaking, on behalf of all of us here at *Let's-Go* we'd like to wish you all a very pleasant journey and happy holidays." I groaned as the familiar tinkle of my mum's favourite Christmas song began to play out of the plane's speakers.

Drew laughed and we chatted idly about the company and the upcoming conference for a while as a flight attendant walked the aisle, topping up our prosecco, surprisingly I was even enjoying the conversation. I explained that I had recently worked my way up to head of human resources and was rolling out a new initiative to encourage more entry-level talent to join the company and he seemed suitably impressed. I'd given up a lot for that job, but I knew that I couldn't hold myself back for the sake of a guy. In the end, my choice had been to move to the states with Seth while he pursued *his* career or to stay in London with *Quinnings* and take the promotion they were offering me. Most of the time, I didn't regret my choice.

By the time we'd moved onto our fourth prosecco, Drew had moved into the middle seat next to me and we watched in amused silence as the woman who'd walked past us about twenty minutes ago headed back to her seat with three buttons mixed up on her blouse.

Her seatmate followed a minute later and Drew and I exchanged a look that made me laugh breathlessly.

"I don't know how they even managed that in the toilets on here, they're ridiculously small."

"You mean, you're not a member?"

"Member?" I asked, scrunching my nose.

"Of the mile high club," he whispered and tapped my nose like I was adorable.

I laughed as I swatted his hand away. "Definitely

not, there's nothing as unappealing to me than banging over a toilet in a cubicle that's barely big enough for my hips and then doing the walk of shame."

Drew grinned. "That's fair, I guess. Remind me to show you how big the bathroom is on my private plane sometime. Maybe you'll change your mind."

I raised a cool eyebrow, this guy was forward and… I didn't think I minded it. "If it's a private plane why would you bother with the toilet?"

He choked on his prosecco as he snorted. "What, you think I've got some kind of Austen Powers disco bed on there?"

"You could," I reasoned. "I don't know you well enough to know what kind of taste you have yet."

"Yet," he mused and I felt a burn of embarrassment sting my cheeks before he smirked. "Well I suppose we'll just have to remedy that, won't we? I'm meeting with a friend for dinner tonight at the lodge, but how about tomorrow? Dinner and drinks?"

"Sure." I smiled and it felt real. "I'd love that."

I was friends with surprisingly few people at the company, so it would be nice to have someone to hang out with, as much as I loved my own company.

"So what exactly do you do at *Quinnings* to get you a private plane? And how do I transition?" I teased and he chuckled. "Or maybe more importantly, why are you flying commercial with the rest of us?"

"Oh well, it's good for the soul you know – don't want to inflate my sense of self-worth too much." He grinned and I rolled my eyes. "A friend of mine actually used to work for the company and thought I'd be a good fit as a new investor, so I decided it would be good to get to know the company and its employees a little better."

I blew out a sharp breath. Crap, he was one of the new shareholders. Well, as long as he wasn't on the board of directors he wasn't technically my boss, I already had enough of those I was lusting after – in a never-gonna-happen way, of course.

"So your job is that you're rich?"

He gave a shrug that drew my gaze to his broad shoulders. "Yep."

"Must be nice," I mused. I did okay financially, but I worked and lived in London. My one-bed apartment ate up the majority of my pay and I'd been thinking about moving out of the city altogether. I used to love being on the doorstep to so many things to do and see and places to eat and shop but the truth was… I didn't utilise any of it. Sure, Seth and I had gone out to see shows and for food all the time, but since we'd split up it wasn't something I'd bothered doing for myself. Yeah, my commute was short. But living in London, one of the busiest places in England, and having nobody to hang out with just made it feel… lonely.

"You okay? You drifted away for a second there."

I smiled as I turned back to look into Drew's concerned bambi eyes. "Yeah, just thinking about work."

He gave a low whistle. "Good to know the staff are dedicated then if they're anything like you."

I laughed. "So tell me more about this friend who brought you to us."

"What, I'm not enough for you?" He gave me a mock outraged look before smirking. "I've known him for years, we actually went to college together in the States and he just recently moved back. One of our friends knows the boss, so when he suggested we come into the fold I agreed."

"It's good that you guys have been friends for so long. I never went to uni, most of my friends are old work acquaintances."

"We kind of fell out of touch for a while when he moved back to England after college, so it was great to reconnect. It's nice having someone who just gets you, you know? I don't have to explain the joke to them because they were there."

I didn't know, but I nodded anyway.

"So yeah, Seth and I got back in touch after he'd come back from overseas and—"

I tuned out the rest of his words. There was no way that *his* Seth and *my* Seth were the same person. Right? How could he have a close friend that I'd never met or even heard of before?

"Sephy?"

"Hm?"

"Are you… okay?"

"Oh, yeah, fine. Just tired, you know, early flight." I laughed to cover my babbling and Drew eased back against his seat with a nod.

"That's who I'm meeting tonight, actually, Seth

and my other friend from college. He worked for *Quinnings* before actually, I wonder if you guys worked together?"

My eyes flew to his before they darted away. Was he being serious right now? Had Seth really never mentioned me to him?

"Oh, doesn't ring a bell," I said faintly and Drew nodded with a little hint of disappointment tugging at his mouth.

Fuck. I'd been flirting and having a good time with my ex-boyfriend's best friend, and he didn't have a clue. One thing was for certain, there was no way I could go for drinks and dinner with Drew now.

CHAPTER 2

Julien

I'd arrived at the lodge two days ago, a full day earlier than most of the employees, so that I could prepare the conference space and make sure everything was ready. This was my first time leading the retreat in my father's stead and it had to go perfectly – though sometimes I wondered why I bothered. This was an annual retreat and I hated it every single year, somehow I doubted that feeling would get any better just because I was the one running it.

"Yes, everything's in place. Relax. I've got it under control." I kept my voice smooth and calm even as frustration boiled inside me. Why had he even asked me to run this thing if he didn't trust me to do it? "Dad —" I listened patiently as he rattled off another checklist and I clenched my jaw so I wouldn't interrupt. "Yes. Okay. I've got it. I'll call you later."

I finally let out the deep sigh that had been building as I slipped my phone back into my suit-jacket's inner pocket. I loved my father but he was a complete control freak, a trait I had inherited and found more than annoying when it was directed at me. *He's just trying to be helpful.* I didn't mind running the retreat, really, or even running his company. It was just that… Well, I kind of hated it. Hated the job, hated the pressure, hated that I had no *control* even though I should have had it all.

Tugging my tie straight, I rounded the corner from the main conference room and stopped in my tracks as a figure lingering by the reception desk spotted me. I instinctively smiled and then let it drop. My feelings about Seth were… complicated right now.

My best friend had no such qualms, striding up to me with a huge grin on his face and clapping me on the back.

"Wondered when I'd bump into you. It's good to see you man."

"Hey," I said lamely and Seth's smile faded a little but I couldn't bring myself to offer more than that as we started walking towards the main entrance that would lead us outside and back to the lodges.

The issue was this: I loved Seth like a brother. We'd graduated college in the states together, worked together, fucked women together, and then he fell in love. This in itself wasn't the problem. No, the problem was that he'd fucked off to the states at the first hint of a promotion and left behind the most incredible woman I had ever–

I shook my head free of the inappropriate

thoughts. Sephy was never meant for me, she was Seth's girl, but he'd fucked things up with her and I hated seeing how heartbroken she'd been for months afterwards. He hadn't had to deal with that fall out, but I had. We weren't as close as I'd like, but that was mostly because I forced distance between us at almost every opportunity. If I didn't, I might be tempted to take her for myself.

"Good to have you here," I said at last, strained smile pulling at my mouth and Seth ran his blue eyes over my face, a slight frown crossing his expression.

"It's been too long. You're coming for drinks with me and Drew later right?"

"Yeah of course." Despite Seth breaking the heart of the woman I… fancied? Lusted after? Fuck, what difference did it make what I called it? It was never going to happen. But despite all of that, he was still my friend and it felt less and less often that we were able to hang out all three of us. Seth and I had gone to college in the US, which was where we'd met Drew, but once we'd graduated and eventually moved back to the UK it was harder for us all to stay in touch. I hadn't minded the distance for the past few months though, not when Sephy had been thriving, not when I loved watching her confidence bloom again. Distance made it easier for me not to drive my fist into Seth's face.

"Good, good… Hey, listen, I was actually wondering—"

Please don't ask me about her. Please, please, please.

"—if you'd seen much of Sephy lately? How's she doing?"

I blew out a long breath but it did virtually nothing to calm my irritation as I pulled Seth to a stop with a firm hand on his arm.

"Leave her alone."

"What?" Seth's jaw ticked and I ignored it even as I recognised it as probably one of the only warnings I would get before I pushed him too far.

"She doesn't need you to charge back into her life, man."

"And what would you know, exactly, about what Sephy does or doesn't want?" I said nothing and Seth's mouth curled into his most infuriating smirk. "Oh, I see. How long have you wanted to fuck her?"

"Seth it's not—"

"Don't lie to me, Jules."

I clenched my hands as anger pulsed in my chest in waves that made my heartbeat speed up. I loved Seth like a brother, but we fought like it too. Pretty much nobody could push my buttons quite like him. It was like I had a mental trigger labelled *PISS JULES OFF* that only Seth had access to.

"This is a business trip." I let a steady breath blow out as I willed away my anger, opting to ignore his accusation… even if it was true. "You don't need to talk to her. Let me handle that, okay? I mean, you never had a problem with sharing before." The taunt spilled out unbidden and a flash of anger flitted over Seth's face. "Look, all I'm saying is that you hurt her before and I'm not going to let you do it again. Walk away, man."

"Whatever," Seth said at last and I relaxed. "Show me where our lodge is then, arsehole."

The tension between us faded away and I grinned as I flicked a glance down at Seth's shiny business shoes.

"Yeah, sure," I said as we made our way out into the snow and then I doubled over laughing as he bit the dust not two metres out from the hotel's main entrance. He glanced down at the thick snow boots I wore and bit out a curse as he slipped on another patch of ice.

"Come on, bambi." I took his arm in my hand as I tugged him along and kept him upright. "I need a drink."

"Me too." I heard him mutter and I laughed. The air was so fresh here it felt like I could get high just from breathing. The sun was ridiculously bright as it bounced off of the spill of fresh snow and caught on the icicles that clung to the fir trees and Seth stopped when I did, leaning against the fence of the reindeer paddock as we took in the scenery. It was, perhaps, the only thing I enjoyed about these annual conferences and even then, the memory of the landscape couldn't compare to the frost-bitten reality.

I'd always been a fan of the winter, loving how my fingers grew numb and the way snowflakes caught on my eyelashes, the fogging of warm breath against the cold air, a warmer hand slipping into my own, tucking itself in my pocket. For a moment I just breathed, breathed and imagined Sephy was here with me, her hand tucked in mine, her back nestled against my front as I breathed in the sweetness of her hair.

"Let's go, I'm freezing my balls off."

Seth. I sighed, drawn out of the fantasy and walking off in the direction of our lodge as Seth slipped and cursed behind me, his shoes having no traction on the snow-packed ground.

"Do you know what time Drew is getting in?" I asked once Seth had made it up the snow-slick stairs and onto the wooden decking and he glared at me through the wet hair that had flopped into his face, damp from the fresh snowfall and his many topples over into a drift.

"Around noon I think, he was flying in from England."

"How come?" As far as I knew, Drew spent the majority of his time in the States.

"I didn't ask." Seth shrugged and a large piece of snow dislodged from his suit jacket.

"You did bring a coat right?"

He shrugged again. "I don't own a coat."

"You don't *own*—" I shook my head, thinking back to our college days and how more often than not he'd walk around in short sleeves and a beanie… in the middle of a Boston winter. I'd assumed he'd have grown out of it but I guessed the suit jacket was an improvement. "They have winter clothes for hire if you're planning on taking to the slopes."

"Fuck *yes* I am, it's the only reason I came on this trip." He cast me a sly look and I tensed, knowing what he was going to say next. "Well, that and Sephy, of course."

I rolled my eyes as I clunked my boots together outside the door to free them of the snow – I'd made the mistake last night of just leaving them on the floor in the foyer and had walked in an ice-cold puddle of water in the morning. Lesson learned.

The lodge was more than big enough for the three of us, with a sauna on the bottom floor and I'd counted four bedrooms, so we had a spare. It had a kitchen, though I doubted any of us would use it, and at least two of the bedrooms had an ensuite. I'd already claimed one of those for myself and had half-expected to find Seth running through all the rooms like an overexcited puppy as he checked out the digs, but instead he was standing next to the balcony door, staring out at the snow.

"It's much nicer to look at from here," he explained, "where it's warm."

I snorted but didn't disagree. The lounge area was my favourite because it had a huge fireplace and the sofa ran along the length of a large window, the brightness of the snow outside lighting the room and leaving it a cool blue once the sun went down.

"How're things with your dad?" Seth dropped into the armchair next to the fireplace before leaning forward and fiddling with the buttons to turn it on. "Is he coming on the trip at all?"

"No." I let out a short laugh before rubbing the bridge of my nose tiredly. "He's fine, we're fine."

"Sounds like everything's fine," Seth mused and I threw him a disdainful look.

"It is."

"Okay."

"Seriously."

"I believe you." Seth stretched out once the flames had risen, his semi-long hair dripping fat droplets of water onto his shirt.

It was silent for a moment except for the pop and crackle of the fire before I sighed. "Fine, it fucking sucks."

"There we go." Seth's eyes flashed open and he grinned. "He still wants you to take over for him?"

"Yeah." I groaned as I tilted my head back and stared up at the wooden beams of the ceiling. "I think I'd rather die. Like, genuinely."

Seth frowned. "Why don't you just say no?"

"Nobody ever tells my father *no*."

"Maybe you could start a trend."

I sat up and looked out of the window at the snow. "I don't even know how I'd tell him. Like, sorry dad, I know you've been grooming me for this role my entire life but thanks but no thanks?"

"I mean, it could use a little refining but it's a good start."

"He needs me," I said quietly and Seth looked at me, eyes clear and face relaxed.

"No, he doesn't. You're good at your job, Jules, but

he can train someone else. It's your life, you can't live it for him." He leaned forward and rested his hands against his knees. "The company would be fine without you and so will your dad."

"He'll be disappointed," I countered and Seth shrugged.

"He'll get over it."

Maybe he would, but I hated disappointing anyone, but especially my father. I was grateful for my job but I didn't love it. It didn't excite me. But the problem was, I didn't know what else *did*.

"What does Sephy think?"

I looked up sharply and found his eyes on me. There was no hostility on his face or in his voice, just curiosity, and I studied him as I considered his question.

"We don't talk as much as you seem to think," I said dismissively and a corner of Seth's mouth tugged up.

"So she thinks you should quit too, huh." I threw him a withering look and he laughed. "Listen, I'm not mad at you. Sephy is…" His eyes became far away until he seemed to shake himself. "I get it. But *you* need to get that at least for now, I'm here, so you're going to need to play nice."

I rolled my eyes and opened my mouth to reply when the front door banged open and revealed a grinning Drew, his long dark hair wet from the snow and his cheeks flushed pink. "I just met the most amazing woman on the plane," he announced and Seth and I shared a look of begrudging amusement.

"Sephy," we said together and Drew blinked as he hung up his duffle coat.

"How did you know?"

CHAPTER 3
Sephy

Why did this resort only have one restaurant? I was staying inside the main hotel rather than in one of the fancy-pants lodges for the execs but if I'd known I'd need to self-cater I would have put more effort into trying to snag one! I was probably being ridiculous. So what if Drew, Seth and my boss were all sitting at the same table together, laughing? I had to eat just like anybody else but everyone knew that the first time you saw your ex after your break-up was important – going into the restaurant and eating alone didn't really give off the *I'm-fine-without-you* vibes I'd be hoping to project when I saw Seth. But then again, what said *strong-independent-woman* more than eating by yourself and not giving a crap about it?

I thought I'd already dealt with the worst this day could offer when I'd finally got off the plane and the coach had dropped us off at the hotel. Drew had continued to chatter on pleasantly and I'd done my best to hold up my end of the conversation, but it was hard when the whole time I couldn't stop thinking that *he was Seth's best friend* and he didn't even recognise my name – that obviously made me think that it was because Seth just hadn't mentioned me. And what did that say, really, about us, about our relationship, that he hadn't mentioned me by name even one time? It was an uncommon name, Drew probably would have remembered it, so the only other logical explanation was that Seth didn't think about me enough to even let slip my name. So the rest of the plane ride had been awkward for me, even if Drew was funny and charming. Of course, then I'd actually arrived and bumped straight into Eileen.

I didn't dislike very many people, there were even fewer that I hated, but Eileen… She grated on me. All she cared about was gossip and god forbid she caught you in the small kitchen on our office floor, because then you would be peppered with questions and conversation that really, I did not give a fuck about. Like, *did you hear Amanda from IT is getting a divorce? Apparently, he slept with the nanny! Fancy that!* I didn't even know Amanda, let alone that she was getting a divorce – but it didn't matter what the situation was, if Eileen could find a way to make it her business, she would. So I'd had to endure her chatter all the way up to the front desk, then in the lift, and *yay we're on the same floor.* Then to top everything off, Seth was here. With Drew. And Julien. I wanted to ask if this day could possibly get any worse, but I didn't want fate to take that as a challenge.

I was currently sat in the bar and entertainment area that precluded the restaurant, nursing some kind of strawberry cocktail as I debated on whether I could go in there. I mean, I looked fine and I was going to have to see him at some point, but the thought of seeing him there with Drew and Julien too was not appealing. Like, at all. The sound of Seth's laughter reached me even from my barstool and I winced. I'd thought I would be over him by now.

We'd met when I was twenty-three and dated for four years, nearly five, before he decided to leave his life (and me) in favour of a job opportunity abroad. In some ways, I got it but it didn't mean it hadn't hurt. We'd broken up almost a year ago now but old habits died hard and it still hurt my heart to know he was happy without me, that the next time I saw him we would stand at a professional distance and smile politely – like I didn't know what he looked like naked or know that he could quote almost the entirety of *Shrek* from memory alone. Stupid shit, maybe, but it was four years spent together only for him to end up right back where he started.

I downed the rest of my drink and buttoned my suit jacket when I stood. *Room service it is.* I'd hoped this trip would give me back some me-time, a chance to decompress and actually enjoy the holidays for once instead of being surrounded by family drama. Instead, I just felt… sad. I was nearly thirty and something about approaching those digits makes you take stock in your life. I hadn't gone on a date in months, I was pretty sure my vag would be growing cobwebs if not for battery-operated assistance, I had no real close friends to speak of and while I didn't have some kind of five-year goal when it came to marriage or relationships, I did feel notably alone. That was another reason I was glad to avoid my family this year, it bought me some more time to stave off the questions about when I was going to settle down or when I would have kids, it never seemed to occur to my nosy aunts, cousins, or the neighbours next door, that maybe I didn't *care* about those things.

I loved my nieces and nephews and they were disgustingly adorable considering my brother had spawned them, but that didn't mean I wanted to be a parent myself.

"Sephy?"

I froze next to my barstool and then turned very slowly to take in the man standing in front of me. Maybe I would have ignored him if not for the fact that he was my boss.

I pasted on a smile that hopefully said *of course I haven't been drinking at the bar by myself* and couldn't resist looking Julien over. Despite his very off-limits status, he was too good looking to not appreciate. It would be like going to the British Museum and only seeing the bog.

"Hey, how are you? Good flight in?"

Julien surprised me, striding forward and wrapping his arms around me. For a moment my arms hung limply, too taken aback to really reciprocate before they automatically came up and hugged him back.He pulled away quickly, clearing his throat as the tips of his ears flushed pink. "Ah, yes. The flight was fine. I'm glad you made it in alright. Are you coming in for food?" He gestured to the open doorway behind him that led into the restaurant area and I finally composed myself. Sure, Julien and I were friends, we even flirted on occasion, but we didn't… hug. Not that I'd really had a problem with it, he was warm and his arms seemed ridiculously large around me, making my curvy frame seem somehow petite.

"Sephy?" he said again and I blinked, realising I hadn't said a word since we'd hugged.

"Sorry." I gave a strained laugh and his blue eyes ran over me in something like concern. "Just tired, long day travelling. I was actually about to head upstairs."

"Right, sure, of course. Sorry, I won't keep you." He smiled and a fluttering began low in my stomach before he turned away in the direction of the bathrooms and then paused. "Um, Sephy, one last thing…"

"Yeah?"

"Seth's here."

"I know." I bit back my grimace as Julien looked back at me. "I met Drew on the plane, he told me."

"Okay, well… If you need anything–"

I nodded quickly. "Thanks." He bit his lip and as the light hit his face more fully I realised he had dark circles around his eyes. "Is, um, everything okay?" This was veering into dangerous territory, it was a personal question. Probing, even. The problem with Julien was that my brain blurred the lines between him and me enough without me prying into his business and making it worse. Yes, he was attractive. And kind. And funny. And—

"Yeah, everything's fine. It's just…"

"What is it?"

There was a pained look on his face that I'd never seen before, like he was fraying at the edges. Julien was calm and collected, always. Something must really have been weighing on his mind for him to seem so out of it.

"I hate these retreats," he blurted, surprising me and I laughed once, shocked.

"I'm glad for it this year, actually." I smiled and he seemed to relax, like he'd been worried I would somehow judge him or send him on his way with a nod. "What do you hate about them? The weather?"

"No, I love the snow actually." His lashes lowered as he frowned at the floor and I watched him quietly, wondering whether he was going to tell me what was really bothering him. "I hate being here, running this thing. I hate…"

Ah. I nodded understandingly. "You hate your job."

His head jerked up and his icy blue eyes were wide. "I don't…" He sighed. "Yeah. I hate my job."

"So quit."

"Just like that?"

I shrugged. "I mean, HR always appreciates when

you put in your notice," I teased and a smile pulled at his mouth.

"Maybe," he murmured and I cleared my throat when the silence stretched on before reaching out and touching a hand to his arm. He looked at it in surprise and I dropped it quickly, stepping backward so I wouldn't be able to feel the warmth of him on my skin and praying that I wasn't blushing right that second.

"Anyway, I should..." I gestured behind me and Julien nodded quickly.

"Of course, of course. Well, it was good seeing you. Enjoy the rest of your evening."

Loud laughter and footsteps headed our way, the sound of it all too familiar and I knew my face had likely drained of colour. Seth was heading this way. I just wasn't ready to face him yet. I knew I'd have to at some point just... not tonight.

"Thanks, Jules."

Julien smiled a little at the nickname and said nothing else as I strode away, hoping I could make it out of the bar and back to the lifts before Seth or Drew could spot me.

I'd actually been looking forward to this trip before I'd known my ex would be here – and even then, I was still hoping I could make the most of this conference away. Surely Seth and I wouldn't have to interact that much?

I wanted this trip to be the ultimate me-cation. I'd packed a load of sexy lingerie (complete with garter belts and all), as well as my comfiest PJs, a whole range of seriously cute outfits that I'd been wanting forever but wouldn't have been able to afford without my Christmas bonus, and… my new vibrator.

There was nothing wrong with the old one, but I wanted to feel good. I wanted to treat myself, focus on only *myself* for the first time in a long time. I was single and hot and I wanted to pamper myself. Sure, I'd have team-building bullshit to do during the day and a few team dinners too, but the rest of the time I had all to myself. There were at least three shows I'd been wanting to binge for a while and a handful of steamy books that had been loaded onto my eReader months ago and had been neglected while I put all my attention into getting everything sorted in the office for the new year and the new recruitment program. I needed to get my mind off of the three men in the restaurant downstairs and back where it should be – on my self.

In preparation for three weeks of mostly-relaxation, I'd paid a little extra to upgrade my room. It contained a huge bathtub as well as a walk-in shower and I felt like I was living the life of luxury, especially when I looked out the window and saw fresh snow pouring down. I'd devoured the room service dinner (which had been surprisingly good) consisting of stew and red wine and had stripped off to starfish in the decadently big bed. It was piled with pillows and blankets in various shades of purple and the duvet was a cosy shade of coffee a little lighter than the walls of the room. It was almost exactly what I'd been hoping for when I'd daydreamed about this trip for the past couple of months.

Despite my heartbreak, things in my life had been so good since I'd chosen to stay in England without Seth. I got my promotion, and running the department had been everything I'd hoped it would. Plus I'd recently been able to custom tailor my own suits, something I'd wanted to do for ages but hadn't had the money for, thanks to my promotion and bonus I'd decided to splash out. I loved a power suit, especially if they were in pastel colours, but finding anything that fit both my thighs and my waist and didn't strain over my bust was nigh impossible. But it was amazing how much of a confidence boost it was to have clothes that actually fit.

I sipped my red wine, swirling it around absently in one hand as I stared up at the ceiling, remembering the warm feeling of Julien's arms around me earlier. It had been… surprising but nice. My mind began to wander, the wine making everything pleasantly hazy as I wondered what it would feel like if Jules' hands had shifted a little lower, stroking the small of my back, smoothing over my arse.

I took another sip and Jules' light blue eyes were replaced by a deep brown, wicked and teasing, full mouth forming the letters of my name so interestingly until I couldn't help but think about what Drew's mouth might look like on other parts of me. Closing over a sensitive nipple, stroking delicately over my clit…

I blinked and realised my hand had followed the pathway of my thoughts and I gulped the last of my wine and put the glass down on my nightstand as I let both hands cup my boobs, my thumbs brushing my nipples as a more dangerous thought wound its way inside my head. The feel of Jules' hands on my body, the way they would grip me and manoeuvre me better for Drew's mouth, the two of them working me into fever pitch.

A gasp caught in my throat as I pinched the nipple and rolled it, sending my other hand out and fumbling at the top of the nightstand and nearly knocking my glass over as my fingers closed around the toy.

These fantasies didn't mean anything. They were both friends with Seth, Jules was my boss, this would never happen in real life.

Satisfied that this was purely about fantasy, about fun, I set the toy to thrumming and my mouth went dry in anticipation.

My old vibrator was fine, it got the job done, and was fairly discreet. This toy had a nozzle on the front and I'd never used anything like it before.

I let my hand drift down over my body, thoughts returning to Drew's wicked smile and how that might look directed up at me as he knelt between my legs while Jules kissed my neck, and pressed two fingers against my clit, feeling it throb with need.

I was surprised at how wet I was, I'd never had group sex and I hadn't really realised it might be a fantasy for me until now. Although, maybe it had less to do with the activity and more to do with the two men I was thinking about. *Just a fantasy,* I reminded myself and then brought the toy to my centre, not sure what to expect and gasping at the air pressure that settled over me and my hips began to roll.

Would Jules be a dirty talker? No, probably not. But Drew... yeah, I could picture that. I let out a soft moan as I imagined both men's hands on me, their mouths kissing and licking, fucking me until all I could do was–

I moaned and let the toy fall away from my pussy as the muscles in my legs shook from where my hips had arched up off the bed.

It was just a daydream and that was for the best, because if I ever did take Drew and Jules at the same time... I didn't know if I would survive.

CHAPTER 4
Seth

I'd been in Lapland a full day and a half and all I'd gotten for my trouble was a lecture from my best friend and spectacularly drunk at dinner. I hadn't had a single glimpse of Sephy, though I'd thought I'd spotted her last night by the bar but Jules had insisted I was wrong. Not that I was sure he'd tell me if it had been her with his earlier warning still ringing fresh in my ears.

The thing was, I couldn't even fault him for liking Sephy. Yeah, she was my ex, but I'd never placed importance on that sort of thing before, especially not when we were at college in the States. He was right, I'd never had a problem with sharing in the past. I wasn't even really sure I had a problem with it now – in all honesty, the thought of Sephy and Jules together was hot as fuck. Plus, of course, now Drew was infatuated too and I'd always enjoyed sharing the most when it had involved all three of us. Nobody was lonely and nobody was left out, it all just… flowed. I couldn't really imagine Sephy being game for anything like that though, she was great in bed but she often got flustered and I suspected having all three of us there might be overwhelming.

The errant chatter in the small conference room had begun to get on my nerves when the woman at the front clapped her hands together for our attention. Team building crap wasn't my thing, but because I was technically new to the business I had to go through the motions of pretending to care at the very least. Of course, Drew didn't have to do this bullshit. Lucky git was in a meeting with the other investors and the board, which meant I was all by my lonesome.

The noise faded as the woman beamed cheerily at us. She was short and curvy with a gap in between her front teeth and tight curly hair that gave her this highly energetic vibe, it made me tired just watching her. I hoped they were paying her a lot to be wrangling a room full of reluctant adults and making them 'bond'.

The door swung open, cutting the woman's introduction short as someone hurried into the room. A familiar blonde head that made my breath catch.

I knew the exact moment she wished she hadn't bothered coming, because it was the same moment she realised the only available seat was the one next to me. Her baby blue eyes widened adorably before she bit her lip, walking over to me and dropping into the seat I pulled out without a word. Sephy nodded to the woman at the front of the room in apology and she continued on her introduction as I studied my ex's profile.

Was it possible she'd become more beautiful since the last time I'd seen her?

Jules had told me to stay away, but here she was, practically dropped into my lap and I wasn't scared to admit that I didn't have the willpower to deny myself the chance to drink her in.

Her perfect pouty lips were a glossy shade of pink I wanted to see smeared and her cheeks were flushed prettily, likely because I was staring. I should look away. *In a minute.*

She leaned closer to me and I stiffened in surprise as her flowery perfume washed over me, achingly familiar. "Take a picture. It'll last longer."

I snorted and her hair fell across the side of her face when she turned away from me and I instinctively tucked it back behind her ear, freezing when she did and pulling my hand back quickly. I'd been in love with Sephy for years, a small touch like that felt easy as breathing. *But she's not yours. Not any more.*

It wasn't the first pang of regret I'd felt over that fact, but it did feel like a keener sting now that she was here, within reach but still so far.

"Sorry," I murmured and she shrugged like it meant nothing, like she'd barely noticed the brush of my skin against hers. This was going to be a long hour. "It's good to see you," I said once the cheery woman at the front had finished speaking and Sephy's head snapped up, her eyes narrowing as they searched my face.

"Are you being serious?"

I drew back. "What? Yes, of course. Why wouldn't I be glad to see you?"

She snorted and tipped her head back, unwittingly drawing my gaze down to the slightly visible curve of her breasts peeking out of the scoop of her blouse. I swallowed thickly and tried to pay attention to what she was saying even as my dick stood to attention. *This was bad.* I shouldn't be hard for her right now. We weren't together, not any more. Yet, one glimpse at her boobs and my boxers were uncomfortably tight, like my body wanted to make up for lost time and wasn't being shy about letting me know what it wanted.

"Are you even listening to me?"

I blinked, hastily lifting my eyes to meet Sephy's. Her lips were pursed in a pink pout that wasn't doing anything to help my hard-on but it was sadly a look I recognised, and if I didn't get my shit together immediately, I was going to lose this chance to speak with her.

"Of course," I said smoothly and one pale brow lifted as Sephy regarded me doubtfully.

"So you agree with me, then?"

"Right." I nodded for emphasis and her bottom lip twitched before her mouth spread into a full smile that I could have sworn made my brain short circuit as she laughed.

"I'm glad you agree that *It's good to see you* is a lame-arse line and that you're a prick." She snickered and I choked around my laugh. We'd always been comfortable around each other, it was one of the things I'd loved most about Sephy – that with her I'd never had to pretend to be anything other than who I was. That feeling, that easy banter, was still there, but she seemed… different. More confident.

I cleared my throat again as a tingle shot its way down my shaft. The confidence, the new look – well, it was really fucking hot.

Chatter broke out all around us, louder than before and Sephy and I looked around guiltily, realising we had no idea what we were supposed to be doing in the session. The cheery woman spotted the cluelessness on our faces and dashed over, bright smile taking up half her face and I wanted to laugh as Sephy eyed her warily.

By all measures, I was an extrovert – but if *I* found this woman to be too much, then god knew what Sephy was thinking.

"Hi guys! Saw you chatting over here which is *so* great! I love seeing people really get to know each other in these sessions." She blew a piece of curly brown hair out of her face and her cheeks flushed a light pink that was just about visible on her amber skin as she looked at me.

"Oh, Seth and I know each other *really* well," Sephy said, shifting her chair closer to mine and my mind went blank. I should say something. Was she trying to tell me she still wanted me? That she knew I'd made a mistake and wanted to let me fix it?

None of that escaped my mouth, however.

"Yeah," I croaked and the peppy girl's smile dimmed a fraction as she handed over a piece of paper with a set of questions for us to go through with each other.

As soon as the woman left, Sephy moved farther away and I felt dizzy with whiplash. What the fuck had just happened?

"Okay, did I miss something just then?"

Sephy looked up at me, an odd look in her eye. "I don't know what you mean. Now, let's just get on with doing this." Her unspoken *so you can leave me alone* made me feel a mixture of both sad and angry – not at her, but at myself. I was the one who'd screwed up our relationship by leaving, by putting my career ahead of hers, I couldn't just expect her to welcome me back with open arms just because I was here. For all I knew, she could be seeing someone else already.

The thought made me scowl and Sephy's nose scrunched up in concern as she watched me, watching her.

"Everything okay?"

"Are you seeing someone?"

She stiffened. "I don't see how it's any of your business." My jaw stayed clenched until she let out a sigh. "But no. Now, can we please focus on the list of questions? I don't want to suck if she tests us at the end."

Now that was such a Sephy-like thing to say that I couldn't hold back my grin, it had nothing to do with the overwhelming relief that flowed through me when she'd confirmed she was single.

That doesn't mean she wants anything to do with you.

True. But maybe…

"What would you say your biggest weakness is?"

I chuckled. "Wow, going straight for the jugular, huh." I propped my chin in my hand as I leaned against the table, it was some kind of cheap marble vinyl that was vaguely sticky against my skin as I rolled up my shirt sleeves and then folded my head back down. Sephy had stilled next to me and I glanced up curiously to find her eyes on my forearms.

I bit back my grin. She had always liked my arms, and I'd been working out a lot in the last year, needing somewhere to put my excess energy, especially as I wasn't fucking it out while I was still too hung-up on my ex. On *her*.

"Probably Victoria Sponge."

"What?"

"My greatest weakness," I explained seriously. "Victoria sponge cake. Raspberry jam, not strawberry though." I grimaced, the strawberry stuff tasted like overly-processed crap.

"I don't think that's the kind of—"

"Next," I insisted, waving her on. "Or do we need to do you first?"

She looked at me sharply, colour rising to her cheeks and flushing her chest.

I couldn't hold back my grin that time, huffing a quiet laugh as she turned even pinker. "Do your questions, I mean."

"Oh. Oh, yes, of course." Sephy looked away, shuffling the paper around as she cleared her throat and bit her lip.

It told me at least one thing: she still wanted me.

I could work with that.

"So what's your biggest weakness?" I said, leaning a little closer so I could see the fine dusting of freckles across her nose and on the arches of her cheeks. "Other than deep-pan pizza."

A smile curved her full bottom lip and I wanted to bite it, knew she'd noticed my eyes lingering there but couldn't bring myself to pull them away just yet. I blew out a long breath and sat back as she tapped the end of a pen on her chin while she thought.

"I'm a pushover," she announced and I startled.

"Really? I don't think—"

"No," she said and then smiled nervously. "It's okay, I am. It's something I've been working on – standing up and advocating for myself, speaking my truths into the world. If it wasn't for you, for *us,* I don't know if I would have figured that out."

When she'd decided to stay, I realised.

"You seem more confident," I said quietly and this time her smile was wide and so gorgeous it hurt to breathe.

"I am."

The mood suddenly felt heavy, so I grabbed the

paper out of her hand, ignoring her protests as I read aloud. "What's your biggest strength? Well, that one's easy, I can do this thing with my mouth where—"

Sephy snatched the paper back and I laughed, she didn't say anything and I hoped it was because she was thinking about just how talented my mouth could be.

But when her eyes met mine, there was a slyness in them that surprised me.

"I can put my legs behind my head."

I blinked. "What?"

She smiled innocently. "Yoga. I started classes a couple months ago. I'm very flexible."

All of the blood rushed out of my head and I swallowed hard.

"Sephy–"

"Alright everyone! There were some great discussions happening there, it's so nice to see you all chatting! I've got one more quiz for you to do and then we're done for this session." The woman passed around more sheets of paper, this time not lingering at our table, before settling down at the front of the room again as conversation resumed.

I wasn't sure what to do or say. Did Sephy want to pick up where we left off? Or was this just gentle flirtation, force of habit?

Sephy looked over the new questions for a second before putting the paper down with a sigh. The teasing smirk on her face had disappeared and I opened my mouth to speak when she beat me to it.

"Drew asked me out for food and drinks tonight."

I didn't know what I'd been expecting her to say, but it wasn't that. Drew had already told me and Jules about the dinner he'd set up with the 'girl from the plane', he'd been equally surprised and amused when I'd explained who she was. Drew had already asked if I was good with it, and I was so long as it was what Sephy wanted too.

"I know."

"Oh!" Her eyes were wide and I couldn't help but smile a little at how intensely she was analysing my expression. "Once I knew who he was I obviously wasn't going to go—"

"Why not?"

She blinked. "Um, well, you know. You guys are friends, I don't want it to be weird."

"If Drew wasn't my friend, would you have gone to dinner with him?"

She nodded hesitantly.

"Then you should go."

"But he's your best friend, wouldn't it be weird for you both?"

I shrugged. "No. It wouldn't be the first time we'd shared a woman."

Sephy's plush lips fell open into a round O shape that made my thoughts turn a little more inappropriate. She clearly didn't know what to say and that was fine, I'd never brought it up to her before because I wasn't sure how she'd feel about it and I definitely didn't want her to think there was any kind of expectation there.

"Look, if you want to go to dinner with Drew you should. He's a good guy, you'll have fun together."

"Okay," she said in a slightly dazed voice and I bit my lip on a smile.

Maybe this trip wouldn't be so bad afterall.

CHAPTER 5
Sephy

It wouldn't be the first time we'd shared a woman. My head was reeling. Not because the thought of Seth and Drew together with another woman–I felt my face flush redder. It didn't bother me. More worryingly, it did… intrigue me.

I'd escaped the conference room as quickly as I could once the session had finished, not wanting to linger and be forced to make small talk with Seth or anyone else there. We'd been in there for two whole hours and that was just more than enough socialising for me for one day. I'd planned on recovering by having a long bubble bath and a walk in the snow afterward, maybe visiting the reindeer but now…

Why can't I? Just because my brain is fixated on a threesome?

I blew out a frustrated breath and pulled my head out of my hands as I looked out of the window to my left. This was the complete opposite of what I'd been hoping to do on this trip. I was supposed to be focusing on *myself*. Taking care of my needs, my wants. My mind flashed back to last night and the *needs* I'd taken care of then. I frowned. No. No. *No.* There were a hundred reasons why it was a bad idea to go out with Drew tonight, and I definitely couldn't keep fantasising about my boss either. Both men would cause me nothing but trouble and Seth… Well, I wasn't sure that going there again would be a good idea. Had my heart hurt when I'd seen him there? Yes. Would I probably always love him? Undoubtedly. But that didn't mean that I should allow anything to happen between us.

I rubbed my forehead, annoyed that I was obsessing over dates and stupid boys instead of work and relaxation. The snow outside had slowed down, now only a gentle flurry instead of the deluge that had been pouring out of the sky when I'd woken up, it had looked so beautiful, so serene, that I'd had trouble pulling my cosy body out of bed and into the shower.

"Are you okay?"

I tried not to jump and failed. I'd become so engrossed in the snow that I hadn't even noticed anyone approaching – *Quinnings* had hired almost the entirety of the resort for the next three weeks, it was an extraordinary expense and was likely an effort to show off. But hey, as long as they still paid my Christmas bonus, I could care less about what they spent their money on. Though, I was sure they'd likely try to sneak this in as some sort of tax write-off somehow – dinner with clients. I snorted to myself before looking at the young woman who'd taken a cautious seat in the plush armchair next to mine.

Everyone else had to be off skiing or in meetings, I'd been surprised to find this cosy hearth area deserted – well, it *had* been anyway.

"Sorry, it's just… you ran out of the session pretty fast and you looked…"

Freaked out? Shocked? Confused?

"...concerned," the woman diplomatically settled on and I smiled slightly as I recognised her as the instructor from that morning.

"I'm alright, thank you. I just didn't expect to have to spend time with my ex that early in the morning."

She winced. "Ah. Sorry about that, I didn't know. So you and he…?"

I hadn't missed the interest in her eyes earlier, had no right to be pissed about it, but the territorial urge to tell her to *back off* had been there all the same. Seth, as usual, was absolutely oblivious to any female interest turned his way.

I shrugged. "It's complicated." Ugh, I sounded like a cheesy 2012 social media status.

The woman – I realised I either had missed or hadn't paid attention to her name – nodded her head sympathetically. "I'm sure you guys will work it out."

Maybe that was what I was afraid of – I liked who I'd become after Seth had left, after I'd chosen to stay, and I didn't want to undo all of that hard work I'd put in. Maybe that was thinking too lowly of myself, I wasn't sure, but more than that… I was still hurt. Regardless of how much

I understood his reasons why, Seth did still choose to leave me. He was the one who walked away. I wasn't a priority for him and I didn't want to ever feel like that again.

Something of my mood must have shown on my face because the instructor patted my arm. "Do you want to get a drink?"

I raised my eyebrows in surprise. "It's 11AM."

She shrugged and her curly hair bounced with the movement. "So? We're on holiday and it's basically Christmas. We can put it in a hot chocolate if that makes you feel better."

A small laugh escaped me as I looked at her, trying to work out if she genuinely wanted to talk to me or just felt bad that I looked upset. There was a sparkle in her brown eyes that didn't look much like pity, in fact, it looked a lot more like *fun* and I couldn't really remember the last time I'd had any of that.

"Okay," I said, standing up and buttoning my purple blazer. "Let's do it."

She grinned. "Excellent. I knew any girl wearing a matching purple power suit had to be a good time."

I laughed again as we walked away from the windows and down the stairs towards the main bar. "You're clearly a great judge of character." I bit my lip. "I'm probably going to sound like an absolute dick, but, erm, what's your name?"

Her eyes went wide. "Oh crap, I'm sorry. I'm Noel. I should have introduced myself sooner, I think you missed it when you came into the session."

"That's pretty." I smiled at her and she smiled back, leaving a warm feeling in my chest. I'd forgotten how nice it could be to hang out with someone and just chat. I'd been working hard lately, but now I wondered if maybe I'd been working a little *too* hard. "I'm Sephy."

"That's unusual, I like it."

I tried not to cringe. People always said the same things when I told them my name, some kind of iteration of shock, incomprehension, some people just assumed I'd said my own name wrong and decided to call me *Steph* or something similar.

"My mum's a Greek mythology nut, but she thought *Persephone* was too 'in your face'." I drew air quotes in the air, the same way I did every time I recalled the story and Noel just smiled.

"I guess my parents just really liked Christmas? I was a December-baby, to be fair to them."

I chuckled as we picked stools at the bar and swivelled around so we could look out at the scenery as we talked. "Well, I think Noel is nice. My brother hates his name, my mum somehow convinced my dad that Ajax was a suitable name for a baby boy."

"That's definitely a bit of a mouthful."

I grinned. "He goes by Jay." We both laughed a little as the bartender came over. "Do you work for *Quinnings*? Or are you just here for the conference?"

Noel smiled at the bartender after placing our order and he smiled back, somewhat flirtatiously, and I waggled my eyebrows at her when she turned back around.

"What?" She shrugged. "I'm here for nearly three weeks, a girl has needs." I giggled with her for a moment, going quiet when our boozy hot chocolates were set down in front of us and sighing at the first sip. "Yeah I'm just a temp, but I heard there's new positions going with this new programme or something for graduates so I'm going to apply."

I perked up, blowing gently on my drink before I took another drink. "Oh really? Is there a specific department you want to get into?"

Her fingers tapped on the glass mug errantly as she considered my question. "I don't know, I mean, I love what I do now. So maybe something within like, training and development?"

"So part of HR," I mused and she shrugged.

"Yeah I guess."

We chatted idly for a while, ordering another drink as she told me about graduating a year ago but struggling to find work in London.

"Everything's just so saturated," she complained and I nodded in agreement, it was why I'd set up the new programme – finding entry-level work that was *actually* entry-level was becoming close to impossible recently. *Quinnings* was more than happy to let me run the initiative if it meant getting the best new talent, plus with the apprenticeship scheme under way they also got more tax breaks.

I put my glass back down on the bar and reached

into my pocket for a business card. This hadn't been a business meeting really but Noel was… nice. I hadn't realised how much I'd needed a friend until she'd sat down. But in business, it was all about who you knew.

Noel waved me off, clearly thinking I was reaching for cash or my phone to pay.

"No, no, this one's on me. You can get the next?" She smiled hopefully and the gap between her teeth made her seem so cheerful that it brought a grin to my face.

"I'd like that," I said as I pulled out the business card. I'd been so excited when I had them made, they were black and matte and simply had my name and contact info on one side and the *Quinnings* logo on the other. I was almost thirty, but somehow it was having business cards that made me feel like a 'grown up'. "But this is actually for you. Apply for whatever job you want but give me a call in January too, once we're back in the office. Katie's our T&D head and she's amazing, I'll introduce you."

Noel's eyes had bugged out as she read the words *HR Director* on the back of the card. "Oh! Wow. Thanks so much, Sephy. You really don't have to do this. I was looking for a friend, not an interview."

"I know." I smiled at her as I stood up, it was nice talking to her but my social battery was still somewhat drained from earlier. "But why not have both?"

She sprang forward and pressed a kiss to my cheek. "I'll text you later, we can have drinks again."

I thanked the bartender and nodded at Noel. "Cool, sounds good."

Noel waved a cheery goodbye before turning back to the bar, probably to flirt with the guy behind it a little more and I snickered as I got in the lift to my room. I thought some fresh air would do me good, it wasn't often that I got to spend time in the outdoors besides the parks in London.

I tugged on the snow boots that came with the room and held my foot out in front of me gingerly. They were black and blocky, the absolute opposite of anything I would pick out for my own wardrobe that was generally a riot of colour. But by the time I bundled up in my coat, scarf and gloves out in the snow, I was grateful for them. My regular boots were cute, a soft grey with fur inside and a grippy chunky heel, but I would have been on my butt in two seconds flat in them. In fact, there were a couple of deep spots in the snow as I walked toward the reindeer that showed places where someone had taken a tumble, the shape of an outflung hand accompanied by a long white line leading up to the dip.

It had been forever since I'd seen the snow. Despite it being freezing in London, it was actually too cold for it right now, and even if we'd seen some I wouldn't have been able to enjoy it. In London, all the snow meant was inconvenience – delays, soggy socks, errant snowballs that were probably more ice than powder. This was wholly different. I'd never been on a snowy holiday before and it was so… quiet. Some people had opted to bring their families with them on this conference trip, mostly those with kids too young to leave behind and who didn't want to miss out on Christmas day antics, but even so, everything felt calm.

The main building housed the hotel, restaurant and conference rooms, but branching off from there were snowy pathways that led to the lodges, slopes, and the reindeer. I followed the handy signs until I stood near a wooden fence, able to stand there and just watch them. The cold stung my nose and I couldn't wait to have a soak in the bath once I got in and thawed out my toes, but they were beautiful creatures. Their coats were thick and looked like they'd be soft, and up close they were really quite majestic. There was even a baby one lurking at the back and I smiled as more of the reindeer came and stood near the fence panel in front of me, sticking their heads out at me and huffing into the cold air.

"I wondered what they were so interested in that they ditched me, but I guess now I understand. Pretty lady trumps food, I guess."

I glanced to my left as Julien stepped up beside me and smiled. "You brought food?"

"For the reindeer, yeah. There's a gift shop that sells things for them."

"What do they eat? Carrots?"

Julien chuckled. "I don't know, they gave me this cone with stuff in it. I think it's oats? They seem to like it." He held out one lightly-tanned, long-fingered hand and scratched the reindeer closest to us under its chin. "You can touch them, you know. They're very soft."

I stretched out a tentative hand as another reindeer moved closer and mimicked Jules' movements. "Wow."

"I know."

I'd moved closer to him without even realising it, subconsciously craving his warmth, and the pleasant smell of his aftershave was soothing. I smiled up at him, squinting a little as the sun bounced off of the snow.

Julien fed the reindeer a little more, holding his hand flat and then grimacing at the wet streak in his palm afterward, making me laugh and his eyes glint mischievously.

"No!" I shrieked as he grinned, thrusting his slobbery hand out like he would wipe it on me, he laughed as I stumbled away and our legs tangled as I slipped on the icy snow. The reindeers watched us in something like baffled boredom before walking off, sensing there wasn't any more food as I accidentally brought us both to the ground. Julien rolled to take the snowy impact, white puffs blowing up into my face as I landed on top of him, his hands on my waist and mine curled on his chest. Our faces were so close our noses brushed and I hoped he thought the blossoming redness in my face was from the cold.

He was breathless as he laughed and my eyes dropped down to the tug of his lips as they curled. This was bad. I needed to get up *now.* It had been about two seconds too long to still be lying on top of my boss in the snow.

"Sorry about that," he said, still smiling as I scrambled up and off of him, ignoring how firm his arms felt under my fingertips and trying not to slip again as I moved too fast. "Whoa, easy—" My legs seemed as if they were sliding in different directions and I wanted to scream in frustration, this was not the professional picture I was trying to paint.

Jules' large hands wrapped around my arms, holding me upright as I crashed into his chest, my face smooshed against his navy coat for a second until he pulled back and looked down at me. The cold air fogged between us and his lips parted, eyes focused on my mouth, and butterflies seemed to erupt somewhere lower than my stomach as my pulse hammered in my throat.

"I—" I cleared my throat as I took a slow and deliberate step back. His hands tightened on my arms for a second before falling away. I knew I had to look a mess right now. I could feel the heat in my face and was surprised it wasn't melting the snow that had begun to fall heavier around us, catching in my hair. "Thanks," I said quietly and then bit my lip. "I should probably get back inside before I fall again."

"Right," Jules said. "Yeah probably."

Neither of us moved. The snow and wind picked up speed and I shivered when he stepped closer.

"Do you want me to walk you in?" His voice was low, husky, and when he licked his lips against the cold,

I knew it would be a very, very bad idea to let Julien get anywhere close to my bedroom door.

"It's alright," I managed. "You should head back to the warm."

"Okay," he said, but his blue eyes were still watching me like he had a question to ask.

I took another, reluctant, step back. "I'll see you later."

He nodded, not moving as he watched me walk away. I glanced back twice, unsure if I'd made the right decision in leaving my boss standing in the cold.

CHAPTER 6
Drew

I hadn't been sure that Sephy would turn up tonight – but there she was, looking even more stunning than she had on the plane yesterday. Her blonde hair was smoothed into waves that reached a little below her chest and her blue eyes were wide as she took in the restaurant, nervous.

I smiled and stood up from my seat, waving to her, and she looked relieved to spot me, her shoulders slumping down like the sight of me relaxed her. Yeah, that felt as good as it sounded.

"Hey." I pulled out the chair opposite mine and kissed her hand as I took it to help her sit down. Her curvy body was poured into a red dress that emphasised her waist and the curve of her breasts and I felt my mouth go dry when she smiled back at me. "I wasn't sure you'd come." *Fuck.* I hadn't meant to bring it up, my goddamn mouth-to-brain filter just didn't work sometimes. I didn't want her focusing on any potential weirdness. I wanted her to be thinking about here, now, *us*.

Sephy stiffened slightly but just gave a light shrug in response. "I've been wanting to try out the restaurant anyway."

I gave a quiet chuckle and she relaxed again. "How has the trip been for you so far?"

"It's only been a day," she said dryly, "but fine, I guess. Though I had to pair up with Seth this morning in our team-building session."

"Yikes." I poured us each a glass of water and took a sip before saying carefully, "I know, Seth told me."

"Oh, you've seen him today?"

"We're sharing a lodge – me, him and Jules. Just like old times."

Inexplicably, her face turned pink. "Lovely."

The waiter arrived and I got a beer while Sephy got a cocktail – you could tell a lot about someone from their drink choice. I would probably bet that the cocktail Sephy had ordered would be bright and colourful and suitably sweet and fruity, then I realised I was staring at her while I psychoanalysed her drink choice and blinked several times as I tried to pull my gaze away from her lips, painted a deep red to match her dress.

"So why did you guys decide to share a lodge?"

I shrugged. "It was Jules' idea, we don't get to meet up all together like this very often and I think he was missing me." I tossed her a wink and she laughed. "Are you staying in the hotel?"

"Yeah, the rooms are so gorgeous, you need to see them." She bit her lip as her blush increased. "I mean– I didn't mean to say—"

I chuckled. "No, no, by all means, tell me more about this bedroom I *have* to see."

She took my teasing in stride and I felt heady with relief that the chemistry and ease that had flowed between us on the plane hadn't been a fluke.

The waiter brought our drinks over and I tried to hide my smile while I ordered my food and eyed the explosion of fruit and colour that was Sephy's pink cocktail.

"Do you want to try some?" she asked after the waiter left. "You keep staring at it." Her mouth closed around the tip of the pink straw and I found myself nodding despite never really liking cocktails in the past, too sweet, too fake-tasting. But putting my lips in the same place Sephy's had been proved an excellent motivator.

"Delicious," I murmured before my lips even tasted the drink and she bit her lip. In truth, the cocktail was as awful as I'd expected and I tried not to cringe after my sip… and failed.

"Delicious, huh?" Sephy repeated and I coughed a little.

"Yep." My leg brushed hers under the table and it felt like electricity shot through my body at the slight touch. "Utterly delectable."

She rolled her eyes but there was a small smile curving her bottom lip that made me want to catch it between my teeth and tug. I took a sip of my beer to try and gather my thoughts, as well as clear out that awful concoction Sephy was delicately sipping.

"So how was your meeting this morning? Are you liking the company so far?"

I half-shrugged. "Sure, I mean, it's fine. I'm mostly here as a favour to Jules and Seth, plus I was getting bored of running my own company – that's why I sold."

Food was placed on the table and my stomach growled so loudly that I looked down at it in surprise, half-expecting to find a wild animal under the table cloth. Unfortunately, the food wasn't mine. Sephy laughed and twisted her plate around.

"You can share my chips while you wait for your food."

"Beautiful *and* kind," I said as I munched through one perfectly crisp fry. "Seth was an idiot to ever leave you." An awkward silence descended and I sighed. "I'm sorry, I made things weird again, didn't I."

"Why don't we just clear the air," Sephy suggested and I slumped back in my chair, thanking the waiter as he placed my food down on the table in front of me. "Did you know who I was on the plane?"

"No."

"Okay," she said slowly, cutting into her steak and chewing it thoughtfully for a moment before she spoke again. "Did Seth never tell you about me?"

"I knew he'd been seeing someone before he moved and that he didn't enjoy his new role because of someone he'd left behind, but other than that he didn't speak about you. I think it hurt him to think of you."

She snorted and took a long pull on her cocktail and I couldn't fault her disbelief. I loved Seth, he was one of my closest friends, but *god* he could be an idiot.

"He told me…"

"What?"

Sephy cleared her throat, sipping her drink and looking around the room at the other people dining around us like she wasn't sure she could look in my eyes. "He said you used to share women."

Ah. So that's why she'd looked so… Well, I wasn't sure exactly what her blush had meant earlier, but clearly it had been playing on her mind. "You have questions."

"I guess. Was it more than once?"

"Yeah, we did it a few times."

"It?"

"We were all with the same woman."

"Even Jules?" She looked surprised and I held in my laugh. I wasn't sure where everybody got the idea that Julien was the picture of propriety – I liked dirty talk and a bit of kink as much as anybody but Jules… Well, he made me look like an angel in bed.

"Even Jules," I said dryly.

"I can't even imagine where everything would go," she muttered quietly and I choked on my beer. "How often did you guys…?"

"Pretty often, sometimes we'd do dates together, sometimes it was one-on-one–"

"Wait, you mean you all *dated* her?"

"Yeah." My eyebrows furrowed and then smoothed out as I chuckled. "Oh, you thought it was only sex? No, we were together."

"All of you?"

"All of us."

"Hm."

I couldn't read the expression on her face and truly, I didn't know Sephy that well yet but it kind of looked like *interest*.

"Thinking about expanding your horizons?" I teased and she blushed bright red.

"What? No. No, of course not. I couldn't…"

"Why not?"

She stared at me, cheeks so pink they made the baby blue hue of her eyes sparkle, and shrugged. "I don't know. I couldn't, really. It wouldn't be appropriate. Jules is my boss and you're best friends with my ex."

I smiled gently. "Right. Of course. Silly idea."

She gulped her drink and I felt a sly curiosity raising its head even as I tried to quash it. Sephy might not be ready to admit it yet, but she *was* intrigued by the possibility.

"Anyway," I said, smoothly changing the subject and she looked relieved. "How's your steak?"

We chattered idly, her leg occasionally brushing mine under the table and her laugh making my heart beat oddly, until I found I couldn't look away from her mouth, her eyes, utterly captivated with the way she talked and the animated way she moved her hands as she spoke.

"So you three all went to university together?"

I smiled. "Yeah. Jules and Seth came over from England and I grew up in the area so Boston was a natural choice for me. But a little while after we graduated, they decided to go back home and I stayed in the States. At first we were pretty good about keeping in touch but…"

"Life gets in the way," she said and I nodded.

"And the… women? The ones you shared?"

I hid my smile. I *knew* she still had questions. "What about them?"

"Whose idea was that?"

"It was a joint effort, but really it was her. We all lived together, she wanted us all, we were happy to share."

"And you weren't jealous?"

I shrugged. "No. She liked us all the same and we all had a good time, there was nothing to be jealous about."

Sephy nodded thoughtfully as she finished her drink and I decided to let the subject rest. I didn't want to scare her off so soon, not when it seemed likely that the chance for something amazing might be building.

I paid for dinner while she protested and we walked to the elevator so I could escort her back to her room. "Unless you want to have a walk out in the snow?"

"No," she said firmly, "I've already hit my quota for

falling on my arse today. Luckily, Jules caught me so I had a soft landing."

I tried not to smirk but knew I wasn't successful. She had it bad and either couldn't see it or was in massive denial.

The elevator dinged and the gold metallic doors slid smoothly open. We stepped inside and Sephy hit the button for her floor, her shoulder touching mine as she leaned forward. It also offered me a sinful peek at the full breasts that pressed against her tight dress and I subtly readjusted myself when she stepped back.

"Dinner was nice," she said into the quiet and I nodded, looking down at the top of her blonde head. I was only a few inches taller than her in her heels and I knew I wouldn't have to stoop too much to kiss her.

"I enjoyed it too." I smiled when she looked up at me and her answering lip tilt made my breath catch. I took half a step closer, firmly putting myself into her space and waiting for a moment, checking that this was okay, that she wanted this.

When her head tilted up towards mine, lips parted, I slid one hand under her jaw, marvelling at the softness of her skin against my palm as our noses brushed. The *ding* of the elevator startled us both and she pulled back. I let her go but slid my hand around her waist, tucking her close as we left the elevator and walked down the corridor to a room near the end.

"Thank you." She stepped away and turned to face me and I wondered what she was thinking, never had I wanted to know someone else's thoughts so badly. Did she want to see me again? Was she disappointed I hadn't kissed her?

Her eyes flicked to my lips and then darted back up again and I smirked, watching her eyes follow the curl of my mouth. I slowly prowled forward and pushed until her back hit her door, our breath combining in the fraught space between us until my mouth descended on hers. It was like the slow-building inevitability of lightning during a thunderstorm, her gasp of need wracking my bones and my tongue coaxing hers into a dance that had us both groaning.

Hands fisted in my hair and the palm I had on her waist fell to her thigh as I tugged the leg up and over my hip, pressing us closer together when Sephy murmured her approval.

The sound of the elevator doors closing pulled me out of my head at the same time that a door opened down the corridor and a petite woman peered curiously at us as she stepped into her room. Sephy frowned in her direction, muttering under her breath about gossips as I caught my breath. I didn't want to do this here, in the corridor where anyone might see us.

I carefully placed her leg back on the floor and winced as I readjusted my dick again, it was painfully hard and I knew I would have to take care of this myself later. But she was officially in my blood, my veins, and I stole another kiss, breaking it before I could convince her and myself that she should invite me into her bedroom.

"I look forward to seeing the infamous bedroom," I whispered in her ear, the soft blonde hairs there stirring faintly with my words, "another night."

I pressed another kiss to her cheek and smoothed her mussed hair as I took a step back.

She pouted. "Are you sure?"

"Are you?"

She thought about it for a second before sighing. "Another time."

I grinned, tugging her into one last kiss and moaning when her tongue stroked mine. "I look forward to it."

CHAPTER 7
Sephy

"Now, contrary to what I'm sure you've heard before, trust shouldn't be blind." Noel stood at the front of the large room, beaming at the group of unenthusiastic adults. Her hair was tied up into two buns on either side of her head encircled with cheery red tinsel, it felt like the sort of thing only she could pull off.

We were in what looked like a ballroom or something similar, it had a high glass ceiling and I tried hard not to be distracted by the pretty view of the snow falling down onto the pines that overlooked the hotel. Tried, and failed apparently. It felt like I had only blinked and then Julien stood next to me. I hadn't seen him since I'd left him out in the snow and I had avoided the eyes of both Drew and Julien, as well as Seth, when I'd walked into the room.

Honestly, I was feeling more confused than ever about all three of them. Seth had broken my heart and even if his leaving did make me a stronger person than

I was before, I still would rather have got there slowly, rather than being forced into re-evaluating my whole life when he'd gone. Drew… God, that kiss.

I don't know what had gotten into me last night but Drew made me want to be daring, reckless, and if he hadn't stepped back I probably would have let him into my room and likely had a great time. I didn't normally sleep with guys on the first date, but I wasn't sure what I was hanging onto really – what difference did it make?

My e-reader had glared accusingly at me from my bedside table last night while I'd stared up at the ceiling, too wrapped up in my thoughts to read. Still, while I'd been mentally trying to sort out my circling thoughts all morning, I'd tried my best to avoid the men in my life. Given that Jules now stood next to me as my partner for whatever exercise Noel had chosen for us all, I was guessing my time had run out.

"Excellent." Noel clapped her hands together once and the sound echoed strangely in the room, distracting me from the warmth of my boss standing close to my left. "Now, for health and safety reasons I have put out some matts, but hopefully we won't need them. Like I said, trust should not be blind, it's about clear communication – that's what I want you all to focus on today. So, turn to your partner."

I shifted slightly and was immediately caught by Jules' blue eyes, he smiled and I swallowed hard.

"Label yourselves A or B, person A will be going first."

I raised an eyebrow and Jules swept an arm out with a shrug. Fine. I guessed I was going to be taking the leap.

"Now, person A, I want you to repeat after me: I'm going to fall, will you catch me?" A couple of titters rang out and Noel smiled patiently. "Establishing clear expectations and boundaries is an essential foundation for all relationships, communication is the key to trust. Now, person A, if you please."

I felt dumb. I could see a few other people sharing awkward looks around the large room and looked away quickly as Drew tried to catch my eye. "Jules, I'm going to fall. Will you catch me?"

A muscle in his jaw ticked and his eyes seemed to burn into me as Noel clapped once again. "Now, person B, the choice is yours. This session is about more than trust – it's about setting boundaries, so let person A know if you can accommodate them. Person A, once you have your response, it's up to you whether you choose to let go and trust your partner."

I raised an eyebrow at Noel who just grinned harder. Girl should have been a relationship coach, fuck HR.

Jules re-captured my attention as he brushed his light blonde hair out of his face. "I'll always catch you, Sephy."

So now the proverbial ball was in my court. I eyed him warily. I'd felt the muscles lurking beneath his suit yesterday when we'd fallen in the snow, plus he was a broad guy. While it wasn't something I was ashamed of, I knew I was a big woman. I'd always had curves and thick thighs and a belly, those were parts of myself I'd worked hard to accept and love but it was sometimes hard not to baulk when challenged like this, when you're used to being alienated during these sorts of tests your whole life.

Julien stepped forward, seeing the hesitation on my face. "I've got you."

I supposed I just had to trust that he did, besides, the mats looked soft…ish.

Breathing deeply, I turned around and placed my arms out wide on each side as Noel was now demonstrating for us, then I let myself fall backward. My heart pounded and my mouth went dry and every instinct in my body wanted me to bend my knees, stop my descent, wondering whether I'd hit the mat after all.

Warm hands slipped under my arms, holding me steadily as Jules' body cradled mine. It felt like a flush swept through every inch of me at the proximity, at the slight disturbance of air at the top of my head from where he breathed.

"Nicely done!" Noel gave us an approving nod as she walked past, correcting form and calling encouragement as she moved through the crowd.

Julien's hands slid down the inside of my arms and dropped to my waist, helping me stand, and I kept my back to him for a few moments, willing my blush to die down before I had to face him.

I let out a slow breath and turned, surprised to see him looking as strained as I felt.

"Now, if person A is done, let's swap roles! Remember, don't over commit yourself – I'm sure there are some very unassumingly strong people in this room but a key part of trust is to also know yourself and your own boundaries. Ask yourself, *is this a weight I can feasibly carry?*"

Julien looked me up and down doubtfully and I shot him a challenging look as I crossed my arms over my chest. Now, that was first. When I'd been at school and we'd had to do trust and team building exercises, everyone had just assumed I could, and would, catch them. I was the fat girl, which put me firmly in one of two categories in people's minds: One, I was fat and therefore lazy, unfit, unreliable and would probably drop them. Or two, I was big and therefore sturdy, probably strong, I'd have no trouble catching someone else. Obviously, they were all idiots. Sure, I had a body type that wasn't traditionally coveted—at least not recently anyway, I would have been hot shit in the renaissance period—but that didn't make their assumptions accurate, or any less hurtful.

I widened my stance and held out my arms. "I'll catch you, Jules." The nickname snuck out and his face softened as he nodded and turned.

The other thing those idiots at school had gotten wrong was that I *wasn't* lazy. I worked out, I ate right... mostly. I was just never going to be stick thin, nor did I want to be.

I took a small step back to account for Jules' height and his chest hit mine with a bounce of effort as I steadied him. He quickly regained his footing and turned to me, his cheeks flushed slightly and I took a step closer. His hand settled on my waist and my hand lightly pressed against his chest. The room dropped away, Noel's voice so faint it was almost a buzz as my world became reduced down to Jules, his eyes, his mouth, the way his faintly minty breath tickled my lips.

A sharp clap brought me back to myself and I pulled away sharply, inhaling deeply to try and get the scent of him out of my head. I felt dizzy with want, my skin practically aching as I held myself at a respectable distance from my boss. *My boss.* This couldn't happen. It was a business and HR disaster waiting to happen. Julien had to know that.

Except, the look of raw hunger on his face made it seem like maybe Julien *didn't* know that or, if he did, he didn't care.

"Ah, Mr Quinnings?"

I blinked, pulling my chin out of my palm as I realised every head at the long table was now looking at me. Drew's was the only one that looked amused, probably because he knew what was on my mind all too well. Or, rather, *who.*

The man who'd called my name had a pinched face, old, white, and considering he was part of the board, probably rich. He undoubtedly wasn't used to being ignored. Not that I'd done it intentionally, of course, it was just that these meetings were so… dull. Seth may be a dick, but he was right that I didn't care a lick about this job. If I wasn't so sure it would devastate my father, I would have left a long time ago. *And do what?*

I sighed heavily. "Sorry, could you repeat the question?"

The man – fuck, I couldn't even remember his name, sniffed as his frown deepened. He opened his mouth and I immediately zoned out again as I looked around the room, taking in the faces that lined the table. It was a decent conference room, not so warm that I would get tired, but not overly air conditioned either. It didn't echo, and the colour palette reflected the outside world – browns and greens that were soothing.

Unbidden, my mind returned to Sephy. It had been doing that a lot, thinking of her. Usually at the most inopportune times. It was true that I'd liked her for a long time, but we hadn't spent any great deal of time together. Not until this trip. Not until she was so temptingly close. In fact, I often avoided her in the office whenever I was able. I couldn't get the memory of those blue eyes staring up at me out of my head, the way the snow had caught in her hair and her mouth had looked red against the pale blanket surrounding us. She'd stepped away and if she hadn't, I wasn't sure that I could have. Especially knowing that she'd kissed

Drew. Smug bastard couldn't wait to brag about it as soon as he'd walked through the door after their date.

I ached for her. It was that simple. Feeling her in my arms during those trust falls earlier, turning to find her close enough to devour… it was enough to drive a man insane.

"Mr *Quinnings.*"

A tingle spread through me as I thought back to the way Sephy had bit her lip, stepped away even as she tilted up her chin. My eyes found Drew and narrowed when he smirked. That was it. I had to know.

I stood abruptly and the board members gasped.

"Apologies, gentleman. I have somewhere I need to be. We'll pick this up later."

I didn't wait for a response, buttoning my suit jacket closed as I strode for the door and eyed the lift ahead of me. Sure, I had probably just pissed off a lot of important people. But I felt like I was coming out of my skin, like the very air I breathed wasn't enough to fill my lungs.

I needed to know.

I held down the button until the doors closed and kept on holding so it bypassed the other floors. My foot tapped impatiently against the polished tile and I half-shoved my way through the doors when they opened too slowly.

The corridor seemed to shrink as I hurried through, my long legs eating up the space easily until I stood outside her door, hesitating. Hopefully she didn't find it weird that I knew where she was staying. I was the event organiser, I knew where *everyone* was staying. I couldn't help the fact that I remembered her room number.

I swallowed hard as I stared at the shiny, solid wood and thumped my hand against the door quickly before I could change my mind.

There was a little shuffle and my heart seemed to be trying to pound its way out of my chest. She was definitely in there, I'd hoped as much given that this morning's group activity had been the only one on the agenda. But now that I was here I was realising how rash this was, how wild I'd been. Walking out of a meeting and hurrying up here when really, I had no idea if she wanted me. Maybe I'd been imagining the heat in her eyes, or the way her breath caught when we stood close, or maybe—

The door swung open and my breath left my body as I took her in. Her cheeks were flushed pink and her hair was damp. A silky robe clung to her like a second skin as her hair dripped steadily on to the material.

"Jules," she said and god, the sound of my name in her mouth, touching her lips… I swallowed hard, opening my mouth to say something, anything, when her eyes flicked down to watch my lips.

"Sephy," I finally managed, my voice hoarse as I watched a bead of moisture slide down her chest and disappear beneath the robe. I closed my eyes tightly and only opened them when a light, sweet smell washed over me. She had moved closer, her hand on my shoulder.

"Is everything okay?"

"No," I replied, sounding strangled. "It's not."

I closed the remnants of the distance between us and her breathing sped up, my left arm came around her waist and my right hand fisted in her wet hair as our lips finally, *finally*, crashed together. It was like being able to breathe for the first time without knowing you were breathless and when she moaned my name I wasn't sure I would ever be able to stop.

Sephy's mouth was warm against mine, her body impossibly soft against the firm polish of my suit, and when she bit my lip, sucking it slowly and smirking when she felt what it did to me, I snapped. I picked her up, slamming the door closed behind me with a foot as I whirled her into my arms. She gasped and then moaned when my mouth travelled down from hers and over her throat, nipping and kissing until she was writhing against me, her full breasts nearly spilling free from the robe she'd clearly grabbed in a hurry.

My jacket slid down my shoulders as her hands plucked at my shirt, searingly hot, but I would burn a thousand times over to have this memory, this moment, emblazoned in my mind forever. I'd thought about this a thousand times, all the ways I'd make her moan, but it didn't compare to the reality.

She came alive under my palms, her skin pebbling as her silky robe puddled around her waist and my eyes drank her in greedily.

"Beautiful," I groaned, and she blushed harder, her chest flushing prettily as I dragged my gaze over her breasts and followed their path with my hands, bringing her mouth back to mine before I stroked her nipple. Sephy's answering gasp made me shudder but when she pulled back and away from me I immediately let her go. Thankfully, she wasn't going far.

The silvery robe fluttered to the ground as she slid it off of her body and I went still as I took in her curves, the softness of her stomach and the fullness of her thighs – fuck, I needed those wrapped around my neck as soon as was humanly possible.

I took a step forward and Sephy smirked, shaking her head at me until I froze, unsure. She stepped forward, her blue eyes burning into mine, and my next breath wheezed out of me when she cupped my cock through my trousers.

"You want me."

It wasn't a question, not really but I answered it anyway. "More than anything."

"Then take me," she said, with a cocky raise of her eyebrows and I relaxed, a smile tugging at my mouth. My shirt was already half-off, but I shrugged it the rest of the way, loving the way her eyes caught on the muscles in my arms as they flexed. This time, when I stepped forward she didn't back away, didn't do anything except breathe a little faster and bite her bottom lip.

Her hair was still damp and I tugged on a strand of it just hard enough to make her gasp before placing small kisses under her jaw, making them longer and hotter as I moved down her throat and her head tipped back.

I slowly slid down her body and she watched me breathlessly, lips red from where she'd bitten them and her cheeks pink as she looked down at me. My palms ghosted up and over her legs before settling on the curve of her arse. I gave it a light, experimental smack and was rewarded with wide eyes and a small whimper as I stroked away the small sting.

Moving quickly, I slid my arms across the underside of her legs and lifted her, laughing as Sephy squealed. I pressed her down onto the bed, keeping my weight off her body so I didn't crush her as I pushed one hand one each of her knees, lowering her thighs to either side of her.

She was already wet, glistening for me so prettily, and I groaned as I pulled back and let my chest rest on the bed. Everything about Sephy intoxicated me and the way she was watching me… If I didn't taste her right the fuck now, I would die.

I stroked one hand up her thigh, teasing her as I moved higher and she squirmed on her back, trying to guide my hand where she wanted me. I laughed lightly as I ghosted my fingertips over the outer edges of her pussy and her hips bucked.

"Julien–"

Her voice was a command, but she wasn't the one in charge here. I teased her some more, featherlight touches to her clit that had breathy moans of desperation escaping her lips until I finally pressed down at the same time that I pushed one finger into her. I worked it in and out at half-speed and when she begged me for more, I crooked it, stroking her from the inside as she called my name.

"Need to make sure you're ready for me," I murmured as I added a second finger before repeating the motion. "How's that, angel?"

Her wetness dripped down my fingers and into my palm and the last of my control snapped as I lowered my head and sucked her clit into my mouth, running my tongue over it repeatedly until Sephy's thighs locked around my head and her muscles trembled. I didn't let up and she groaned.

"Wait, Jules, I can't come again—"

I lifted my mouth from her centre, licking the taste of her off my lips as she watched. "Darling, I'm nowhere near done with you."

CHAPTER 8
Sephy

"Jules," I gasped again as he kissed his way back up my body, his tongue tracing the edges of the stretch marks that adorned my stomach and thighs until his mouth closed over my breast and I panted. He moved to the other, nipping and sucking as his hand drew torturously gentle circles over my pussy before bearing down on my clit with the pad of his finger and making my hips rise.

"Yes, angel?" His blue eyes blinked innocently at me, but his lips were curled into a smirk as he made me moan again as he worked me with his fingers.

"Stop torturing me," I begged, biting down on my bottom lip so I wouldn't protest when he moved away.

"I would never," he said as he tilted the metal on his belt buckle, "ever dream…" Julien pulled the belt to one side harshly as he popped the metal hook out and let the belt hang open as he reached for the zip on his trousers. "...of torturing you." He stepped smoothly out of the trousers and I swallowed hard as I realised he wasn't wearing any underwear. The considerable length of him sprang free and Jules tipped his head back as he fisted his cock with one hand, a piece of his blonde hair falling freely onto his face.

Anticipation licked along my skin, making it tingle, as he took a step toward me with an expression of sheer hunger on his face. Warm hands curled under my thighs as he pulled me sharply down the bed toward him and then they climbed my body. I squealed as he flipped me over easily, making my heart flutter from the thrill of it.

"Did you like that, darling?" Jules' hands smoothed over my cheeks, squeezing and tugging until I shifted my hips restlessly and I heard him chuckle. He nudged my thighs further apart with his knees and I felt him against my backside, hot and ready.

One finger pressed into me, curling against the spot that made me see stars and when I moaned he pulled it away.

"I think you're ready for me now."

I lifted my head to peer at him from over my shoulder when nothing further happened and while the heat was still in his eyes, the hardness of his cock obvious, he held himself back.

"Do you want this?"

"Yes," I said, voice hoarse, and I licked my lips as he moved toward me before hesitating once more.

"Shit. Do you have a condom?"

I nodded to the drawer in the nightstand. "In

there." He raised an eyebrow and I fought to keep my blush from my cheeks. "I like to use them sometimes."

Jules bit his lip, eyes darkening as if he was imagining exactly what I used them for. "I'm going to want to see that."

"Another time," I murmured, knowing it was likely a ridiculous thing to say. I wasn't going to make a habit out of fucking my boss, I definitely wasn't going to get myself off in front of him either, but there was only so much pressure a person could take before they exploded.

The foil crinkled as Jules rolled the condom on and then the bed dipped a little more as he leaned down to kiss the back of my thighs, his head nudging at my entrance.

"You have no idea how many times I've thought about this, about you."

The words made me burn with want. It was wrong for us to feel this way. We were breaking all the rules and spitting on the boundaries we'd relied upon for too long, but damn it felt good.

His head pushed inside of me shallowly and I gasped, rocking back to meet him as his hand stroked up and down my back before fisting in my hair and tilting my head up so he could kiss me. It wasn't a sweet kiss. No, it was a clash of tongues, desperation making us dive deeper, moan harder, until Jules thrust inside me in one powerful surge.

His chest covered my back as he fucked me deep, each drag of his cock setting me aflame.

"Fuck," he breathed against my skin as he thrust into me from behind. "You feel so good, so right, angel."

My breath left me in shuddering gasps, Jules' moans joining mine as I clenched around him, feeling my wetness trickling down onto my thighs and his movements became punishing as we each tried to make the other fall off the edge first.

"*Yes*," I called out as his pace quickened and I lifted my hips higher so I could work myself on his hard length. The headboard hit the wall rhythmically and I felt wild, unleashed, like I wanted him to spread me bare so this feeling would never end. "Julien!" I cried out and he echoed me, his thrusts slowing and his hand sliding out of my hair as our climaxes took hold of us.

We were both breathing hard, sweat had gathered between my breasts where my chest had been pressed into the duvet cover and the cool air felt nice on my skin as Julien moved off of me and I rolled over.

The room was quiet, the glow from the lamp on my bedside making Jules' skin look golden and left me feeling surprisingly relaxed. Having sex with someone new was fine, but the aftermath could be somewhat awkward. Yet, I felt just as comfortable lying there naked with Julien as I would have if I were by myself.

He slid his hands under his head as he tilted his face to look at me, a pink flush to his cheeks and a small smile on his lips that I found myself replicating.

"That was…"

"Good?" I ventured and he laughed.

"Everything," he sighed with a smile, eyes slipping closed again.

Everything just about summed it up. I'd always been up for trying new things in the bedroom, and sex with Seth had always been great but there was a roughness to Julien when he fucked that I never would have expected. More than that, I didn't realise just how much I would enjoy it, either.

I stretched my arms out and sat up, pushing my shaking legs over the side of the bed. I would be sore tomorrow, I could already tell.

"Where are you going?"

"To pee," I called back from the bathroom. I did not want to get a UTI. "What did you do with the—" I blinked as Jules appeared in the doorway. He didn't even seem phased that I was sat there on the loo, just deposited the tied condom into the bin beneath the sink.

"Good idea," he said and then smiled as he perched on the rim of the bath. My mouth went dry. Under the brighter lights of the en-suite, it was even easier to see the full gorgeousness of Jules' lean muscles. I cleared my throat and he raised an eyebrow. "What?"

"I'm on the toilet."

"I can see that."

"Why?"

"Why what?"

"Why are you in here, seeing that."

Jules rolled his eyes. "Men need to go after sex too, you know."

"And you couldn't just wait your turn?"

He stood up, mischief in his eyes as he walked over to me. "Maybe I'm just attached to you and don't want to miss a single moment of seeing you naked."

I snorted as I reached for the toilet paper, standing to wipe and then flushing.

"Plus, Drew pees with the door open so I just kind of didn't think about it."

I washed my hands and pointed in the direction of the bedroom. "Okay, well, I'll be out here."

Jules just grinned and I rolled my eyes, hiding my smile as I walked away.

I wasn't sure what was supposed to happen next. Were we supposed to go back to our carefully observed distance? Were we like, fuck buddies? Maybe I didn't need to worry about it right now.

I sank back down onto the bed and beneath the covers, tugging them up to my chin now that my body had gone back to its regular temperature and could feel the cold.

The bed dipped slightly as Jules settled on the other side of me.

"Let's hear it then."

I blinked, turning my head to see him. "What?"

"All the reasons you think that what we just did was wrong."

I gaped. "It *was* wrong, you're my boss and—"

"So, I'll quit."

I felt like I was a cartoon cat whose eyes were about to pop out of their sockets. "*What?*"

Jules shrugged slightly, eyes on the ceiling as if he couldn't feel my stare burning into his cheek. "If I quit, I'm no longer your boss."

I laughed but when he didn't join in the sound cut off, sounding vaguely strangled. "Julien, you can't quit your job for me. That's ridiculous!"

"It's not just for you. I hate it." His jaw clenched and some of my worry dissipated as I remembered the conversation we'd had in the bar the other day. "I know my father wants me to take over from him, and soon, but it's all just so… dull."

I nodded slowly. "Okay."

Julien dropped his hands from beneath his head and rolled on his side to look at me. "Okay?"

"Yeah, if you're not happy then you should leave."

"But my father—"

"—isn't you," I said gently, brushing a piece of blonde hair out of his face. "He'll understand."

Julien smiled wryly and I raised an eyebrow at him in question. "Seth told me the same thing – to quit, I mean."

I nodded, unsure how to respond to the mention of my ex or talk about him with the guy who'd I'd just slept with… who also happened to be his best friend. God, this was a mess in so many ways.

Jules glanced at me and sighed. "It's not weird, you know."

"Julien—"

"It's only weird if you make it weird," he insisted and I rolled my eyes. One warm arm draped itself over my waist on top of the covers and I felt the tension that had been creeping in, fade away. "I don't want you worrying about Drew either."

Oh shit, Drew. I hadn't even got around to worrying about him yet.

"Come to the lodge tomorrow." Jules pressed a kiss to my cheek when he saw my alarmed expression. "They won't be there, they've both got evening activities on the agenda. Come over. I'll cook you dinner, you'll see how easy it really is, okay?"

I wasn't one hundred percent convinced, but I nodded anyway. What was the worst that could happen?

CHAPTER 9

Sephy

It was absolutely freezing outside as I made my way to the lodge Julien was sharing with Drew and Seth, but that wasn't the reason my hands were shaking.

I didn't know what to expect. Julien hadn't stayed over last night, but this… cooking for me, having me over for dinner, it felt an awful lot like a date. I'd talked myself in and out of going all day before eventually pulling on jeans, a jumper, and swiping on some tinted lip balm. I was dressed casually. This was casual. It couldn't be a date if I didn't dress up, right?

I wasn't even sure why it was stressing me out so much. If Julien did decide to leave the company, then there was no issue with me dating him. Was this just the feeling that we were doing something illicit even if it no longer was? Though, he wouldn't be able to put in his notice until after the conference considering he was the one running this thing.

Or maybe I was stressing more about Seth and Drew than Julien.

I walked slowly down the pathway between the reindeer pen and lodges, the snow crunching under my feet as I remained lost in my own thoughts.

I liked Jules a lot already, even if I mostly knew him surface-level. The problem was that I'd also really enjoyed my date with Drew. And Seth… Well, things with Seth were complicated. I couldn't just switch off my feelings for him as if they were never there and, truthfully, I wasn't sure I was over him yet. But all of this was complicated – I wasn't supposed to be thinking about boys right now! And yet, whenever I picked up a book or turned on a show, I found that I'd read the same page over and over or forget what had happened completely in the episode because my mind was just elsewhere.

Did this messy ball of emotions mean going to Julien's for dinner was wrong? I hesitated briefly, the reindeer in the enclosure looking up at me curiously until the snow grew heavier and I hurried on.

I wasn't sure. But it's not like it was a secret that Seth was my ex, or that I'd gone on a date with Drew.

A flush of heat swept through me and I bit my lip, ignoring the blush I could feel climbing my cheeks as I searched for Julien's lodge – number thirty-three.

The wood was wet and a little icy as I stepped up on to the porch and raised a shaky hand to knock. Dinner. It was just dinner.

The door flew open before I could touch it and I

jumped as a widely grinning Drew stared back at me before ushering me in.

"Saw you through the window," he said cheerily, as if he wasn't supposed to be at a meeting with the shareholders over at the hotel right that second.

"Are you on your way out?" I slowly stepped across the threshold and Drew moved back a little but still stayed close, his dark eyes drinking me in like he was starved.

"Nope." He smirked. "I persuaded Jules to let me stay."

Alarm shot through me. "Won't that be weird?" I blurted and Drew moved even closer, the sweet, smoky smell of his aftershave washing over me as he unzipped my coat.

"Not at all. We're good at sharing." He winked and I gulped as he slid my coat from arms and then looked expectantly down at my snow boots.

I toed them off and Drew smiled, reaching down for my hand and intertwining his fingers with mine. Why did I suddenly feel like I was in for more than I bargained for?

Something smelled delicious, warm and tomatoey goodness drifting out toward me and my stomach grumbled a little. Drew chuckled as he tugged me toward a cosy looking leather sofa covered in blankets that overlooked the snowy trees outside. I moved to sit next to him but he tutted, pulling me down and into his lap instead. If he were a cat, I was certain he would have been purring as he rested his chin on the top of my head.

Jules walked around the corner, a tea-towel slung over his shoulder and I couldn't help but fixate on that detail for a moment. I hadn't realised how sexy I would find a man that could cook, but Jules looked good enough to eat. My thighs clenched together a little and Drew chuckled. I flushed, realising he had felt that, and then stiffened as I looked back at Julien. Would he be mad that he had invited me over and I was sprawled over his friend?

"I thought I heard your voice," Julien said easily, he looked between me and Drew, his smile slow before he bit his lip. "Dinner won't be too long. Do you want something to drink? I've got wine?"

I nodded jerkily. "Wine would be good, thanks."

Julien smiled again and I found myself holding my breath as he walked over to me and pressed a warm kiss to my still-cold cheek. "Put the fireplace on, Drew, she's freezing."

Drew lifted me easily, placing me on the leather cushion beside his as Jules went back to what I presumed to be the kitchen. "Don't worry sweetheart, we'll warm you up in no time." Drew's words were innocent but the grin he sent me was entirely indecent and I tried to keep my thoughts away from all the ways they could *warm me up*.

Julien reappeared with a glass of white wine for me and I smiled in thanks as I took a sip. "What are you cooking?"

"Lasagna. I hope that's okay? The local shops were a little limited for options."

"It smells amazing."

Drew plopped back down next to me, instantly draping his arm around my shoulders and tucking me into his side. I gave him a small, amused, glance. Clearly touch was his love language, but I didn't mind. It felt nice to be so wanted.

"So, did you have a good time with Jules last night?"

I stared at Drew. Why would he ask me that? Was he not worried about the fact that I had been on a date with him but then slept with Julien? Unless… maybe he wasn't concerned because they weren't competing. I squinted at him suspiciously. "Yes."

"That's it?" He pouted and my eyes dropped to his full mouth before jerking back up again as he grinned. "What, I don't get any of the juicy details?"

"Drew," Julien said sharply, poking his head around the doorway of the kitchen. "Come and help me bring the food out."

He sighed but stood, giving my thigh a little squeeze before he disappeared around the corner. I could hear their low voices rumbling but couldn't make out any of the actual words. No doubt Jules was scolding Drew, they reminded me of brothers with Drew acting as the rebellious, cheeky younger sibling and Julien the older, responsible one, always in full control of the situation. I blushed, remembering how he had taken control yesterday. Jules was dominant in the bedroom and last night, I hadn't minded that one bit. It kind of made me curious about what the dynamic had been like when they'd shared the same girl before. Was Julien still the one in control?

I cleared my throat, trying to focus on taking in the lodge rather than the dangerous direction my thoughts had spiralled into. It was nice in here, cosy but elegant without being out of touch with the world outside. It made me wish I'd splashed out for the lodge rather than the hotel, but it was far too much space for just one person. Maybe if we did one of these conferences here in the future I could share with Noel, I mused.

Drew and Julien laid the plates out on the long dining table that sat next to the wide glass window on the left hand side of the room, overlooking the snow. Jules pulled out a chair for me and I made my way over, eager to see if it looked as good as it smelled.

Julien sat on my right and Drew settled in opposite me, likely so he could play footsie with me under the table and I shot him a look as Jules dished up the food. I groaned at the first bite, Julien could *cook*.

"This is amazing," I mumbled around another mouthful and he looked amused.

"I'm glad you like it. It was my mother's recipe."

"Wow, she must be a great cook."

"She was." He smiled fondly and reached over to squeeze my hand as if to assure me it was okay that I'd brought her up. I hadn't known his mum wasn't in the picture, not necessarily the best start to a second date. Julien must have read the curiosity on my face because he continued, "I don't remember her really, I was only four when she passed. Car accident."

I nodded slightly. "Still, I'm sorry. It's nice that you can connect with her this way though." I gestured to the food and a small smile tugged at his mouth.

"Yeah, it is." He watched my face intently and Drew cleared his throat loudly.

"Okay, okay, enough about Jules, it's my turn." I raised an eyebrow and he winked. "Don't you want to get to know me too, Sephy?"

I hid my smile around another mouthful of food as I watched him from across the table. "You're right," I said after I swallowed my food. "What made you leave the States?"

Drew's smile dimmed and Julien looked pained, as if this were a topic I should have avoided. Had I put my foot in my mouth twice in a row?

"Bad break-up," he said after a moment and I nodded absently. "It was a while ago now, but I needed a change."

I could understand that, I'd felt the same after Seth and I had broken up.

Drew shrugged. "I thought she was someone else, that she actually liked *me*… turns out she was only really interested in the money."

"I'm sorry." I winced. Geez, that was rough. Not knowing whether someone liked you for you or for what you could do for them had to be hard.

"It is what it is." I'd never seen Drew look anything

other than cheerful, but it was like all his energy had been drained in that moment.

"You deserve better than that," I said with a frown. How many times had that happened to him that he'd just become used to it?

He perked up a little and we resumed eating as Julien glanced between us. The fourth time he did it, I looked directly at him. "What?"

"Nothing." He looked back down at his food and I placed my cutlery down.

"Jules."

He sighed. "I just think it's amazing how well you understand people. You're amazing. That's all."

I felt my face turning red. I didn't normally blush so much but there was just something about these men that affected me differently. Both of their eyes were on me and I swallowed hard, caught between them. I reached for my wine and took a gulp, suddenly feeling too hot, but strangely shivery.

Drew stood, pushing away from the table with ease and Julien looked up at him with narrowed eyes. "Why don't we take a break before we have dessert?" Drew walked around the table and offered me his hand, I took it hesitantly, standing and following him back over to the sofa. He didn't pull me back into his lap and I found I was a little disappointed by that, but he still pulled me close.

Julien settled on my other side, his hand resting on my thigh as he sipped his wine with the other. My breathing felt like it was getting heavier as their warmth enveloped me. I turned to look at Drew and found him already watching me, his eyes dropped to my mouth and I licked my lips instinctively.

One warm hand came up and cupped my jaw and I didn't know whether to pull him closer or push him away. I looked to Jules and found him watching us with undisguised interest heating his blue eyes. Drew tilted my face back towards him, his breath lightly feathering across my lips.

"Do you want me?"

"Yes," I whispered, glancing hesitantly at Jules even as my underwear dampened with want. "But—"

"There's nothing to worry about," Drew soothed. "Jules doesn't mind, do you, Julien?"

"No," a deep voice rumbled and the desire in his voice made my mouth go dry.

"So if you want this, then take it," Drew murmured, his mouth just breaths away from my own. I tilted my chin and his lips brushed mine once, twice, before he kissed me hard, his tongue stroking mine and I moaned breathily.

I'd wondered what the dynamic between them all was like when they shared a woman in bed, and now I suspected I was about to find out.

Drew pulled away, smiling at me and I returned it, hesitantly leaning forward to kiss him again. The hand still on my thigh squeezed a little and I gasped as tingles shot up my leg and made my clit throb.

"My turn," that same growly voice demanded and Drew chuckled as he pulled away, tilting my head to offer me to Jules. "Much better," he smirked before his mouth descended onto mine. Julien kissed like he was claiming, rough and demanding and with no mercy. It was so different to Drew's kiss that I could see how they balanced each other out.

I turned, facing Julien so he could kiss me harder, and Drew followed me, pressing kisses to my neck that had my heart beating faster. Julien's hand stayed on my thigh, stroking and teasing, as Drew stroked from my hip, over my stomach, to cup my breasts and I gasped.

Julien opened his eyes and watched as Drew slipped a hand under my top, cupping my breasts through my cotton bra and rolling the nipples above the material until my hips jolted.

Jules' hand slid higher, like he was competing with Drew to bring me the most pleasure, and as he cupped my pussy through my jeans I panted into his mouth. God, they were going to kill me. But Jules didn't do anything else, just watched me as Drew stroked my boobs and kissed my neck.

"Take those off," Jules directed, nodding at my jeans and I hesitated, looking between them and finding only patience and eager desire on their faces. I stood and unzipped my fly, the weight of their eyes on my skin tightening my breasts and sending a flood of wetness between my legs. I pushed the jeans down and stepped out of them before walking back to the sofa. Julien shook his head. "Those too."

I bit my lip before doing as he said, hooking two fingers on either side of my waistband and tugging my underwear down. I was half-naked, and they each looked like they wanted to devour me. There was a noticeable bulge in Drew's trousers and he readjusted himself with a wince as he looked at me.

Julien patted the sofa and I sat back down. He leaned forward and kissed me again, draining away the tension that had started to creep back into me, and I sighed as I relaxed. Jules pulled away and looked to Drew with a raised eyebrow, he grinned in response and stood up. I didn't have a chance to ask what he was doing before he dropped to his knees.

"He's going to lick your pussy while we watch, okay?" Jules' voice was husky and I clenched in response to his words.

"Okay."

Drew peered up at me, his dark hair was soft against my legs as he kissed his way between my thighs. He wasn't like Julien, who'd wanted to tease me last night. No, Drew's mouth closed over my clit almost immediately and I cried out at the wet feel of his tongue sucking and laving me.

"Add a finger," Julien said off-handedly, watching my expression as Drew did as he asked, working one digit into me and then adding another when Jules directed him. "How's that, angel? Feel good?" I nodded breathlessly and Julien kissed me, long and slow, his eyes molten when he pulled away. "Are you ready for more?"

"Yes," I whispered and Jules shook his head.

"Louder," he taunted and I resisted until Drew

added a third finger, pushing into me relentlessly while his tongue tortured me.

"Yes, Jules, please—"

As if it were some kind of signal, Drew stood up and shucked off his shirt before unbuttoning and pulling down his trousers and underwear until he stood naked. Julien reached down and helped lift up my top and unhook my bra, pausing only to lick my nipples briefly like he couldn't resist the urge.

Drew sat back down on the sofa and we both looked to Julien for instructions. He smiled at us as he reached up and pulled off his navy jumper, letting it drop to the floor alongside his jeans.

"Get on all fours please, darling."

I did as he asked, a little nervous, and he stroked my arse as if he knew I needed soothing.

"Touch him," Julien demanded and I eagerly obeyed, running my hands over Drew's muscular chest and down over his stomach until I reached the trail of hair that ran down to his cock. Drew tipped back his head, his throat bobbing as my hands closed around his base. He was thick enough that my fingers didn't quite touch and a flushed colour darker than the light brown of his skin.

Julien moved around to my other side and reached down to stroke my breasts where they hung between my body and Drew's. "Take him in your mouth, angel."

I licked Drew's tip and he shuddered beneath me, the muscles in his thighs clenching as I wrapped my mouth around him and tried to work him into my mouth. It was hard because he was big and I gagged a little as I took him. I backed off a little and Julien's hand slid into my hair, guiding me down and into a rhythm as Drew's hips began to move in time with my mouth.

Jules pulled away and I realised why a moment later when a foil packet crinkled and I felt him stroking my pussy from my behind.

"Are you ready for me?"

I hummed in agreement around Drew's cock and Jules dipped two fingers into me as if to make sure, curling them until I tried to ride his hand and he pulled away with a chuckle.

I would have been annoyed at his teasing if he hadn't thrust into me two seconds later, spearing me in one move until his hips pressed against my backside and I bounced backwards slightly as I begged him to move with my body.

"You've got to make Drew come before you can come, darling. Think you can manage that?"

In response I slid my mouth down the last little bit, gagging slightly as Drew's cock tested my limits. He moaned my name, his hand fisting in my hair as he held me in place, panting.

"That's right baby, you can take it. You're so good… please," Drew was pleading almost absently but his eyes fluttered open and he watched me as if hypnotised as I glided my mouth up and down his length.

Jules shifted his angle and it felt somehow deeper, fuller, and I moaned around Drew's cock, trying to remain focused on my task even as Jules sent pulses of pleasure through my body. Drew smiled wickedly, like he could see my struggle, and reached for my breasts, stroking my nipples, pinching and rolling them between his fingertips until I was thrusting back against Julien with abandon. The sound of our bodies coming together was caught in between the crackle of the fireplace and Drew's breathy moans as he got closer to the edge.

I tightened around Jules and heard him curse as I pressed my mouth down as far as it would go, swallowing Drew and moaning as he came with a shout, his humps pumping into my mouth as Jules sped up behind me.

I pulled away from Drew and smiled over my shoulder at Jules. His eyes burned hotter and his thrusts turned rough, hard, and I luxuriated in it, stretching back to let him fill me deeper until it wasn't enough. I needed more.

I sat upwards, pressing my back to Julien's front and heard his breathing stutter at the change in position. I took his hand, stroking it down my body until it reached my clit and I circled my hand above his before letting go.

"Jules, please..."

My head fell back against his shoulder, the delicious friction increasing as he pressed down on my clit and a moan tore from my throat. My eyes opened and Drew sat watching us, his cock pressed into his hand, slowly stroking it back to hardness as Jules fucked me.

Julien kissed my neck and suddenly the sensations were all too much – Jules' mouth on my skin, his cock buried in me and his hand working me, Drew's eyes on us as he listened to me moan. I cried out, my pussy clenching as I came and bringing Julien along for the ride.

The motion of our hips finally slowed and I slumped, sweaty and flushed as Julien pulled out and helped me sit back down on the blanketed sofa.

I would have to worry about whether this had been a bad idea or not later, for now, it looked like Drew was ready for round two.

CHAPTER 10
Seth

I'd come home from my meeting to find a pile of clothes in the living room. It was both weird and hard sometimes, listening to your friends get laid while you sat alone in your room – harder still when the girl they were fucking was your ex.

The sound of Sephy's moans carried through the walls and I looked down at my hard-on with irritation. That was the thing that bothered me most of all – it wasn't even that they were fucking the girl I still loved, it was that I wanted to join in and it was never going to happen. Sephy had clearly moved on, and I understood it, but it didn't mean I had to be happy about it.

So yeah, I was jealous. But for all the wrong reasons. This wasn't just FOMO though, I'd known almost instantly that leaving Sephy behind had been the biggest mistake of my life. But I'd been afraid to come back, afraid to see her, because what if she didn't feel the same way? What if she was relieved? Or worse, didn't care at all?

I sighed, swinging my legs out of bed and tugging on my extra layers before heading downstairs. If I stayed much longer I was going to end up having a sad wank or knocking on Drew's door and begging to be let in on the fun. I couldn't see either option being fulfilling.

I tugged on my snow boots and headed out for a walk. There were lamp lights along the main pathway that glinted off of the piles of snow and small fairy lights had been wound around the wooden fence that lined the pathway, making everything twinkle. It should have been romantic, cosy even, and I was standing out here alone. Of course, that was my own fault. If I had never left, maybe Sephy and I would have been on this trip together.

Some of the reindeer still milled around and I leaned against the fence of the enclosure while I tried not to shiver. Snow crunched behind me and I knew without looking who must have followed me outside.

"It's fine Jules, go back inside."

Julien turned to look at me, leaning his back against the fence as his breath fogged the air. "I thought I heard the door slam," he said mildly and I rolled my eyes. Julien was a do-gooder, he avoided conflict like the plague, and the only thing he hated more than disappointing other people was in-fighting.

"Seriously. I'm fine."

"Oh yeah, that's why you're standing outside in the snow at eleven at night."

I shrugged. "I'm still on UK time."

"You are so full of shit. You could have just joined us, you know."

"No, I couldn't." I frowned at him. "She's my ex, you should have seen her in the session we had together. Sephy doesn't want anything to do with me."

Julien clapped me on the shoulder and I winced as the cold made the hit sting. "For someone so smart, you are an absolute idiot."

"What?"

"She still loves you, but you let her down. If you still want her, fight for her."

I sighed. He made it sound so easy. "I don't think there's anything left to fight for."

"You love her, right?"

I nodded, jaw tight.

Jules shrugged. "Then that's what you're fighting for."

"What about you? And Drew? You told me to stay away from her."

"Well that was before I knew what a mopey arse you'd be without her." His teeth gleamed in the darkness as he grinned. "But yes, you'll have to get used to sharing again."

"I think I'll manage."

Julien chuckled. "Good. Fix things so we can all be happy."

"Moving a little fast, aren't we?" I turned to look at

Julien in the low light, scrutinising his face as he answered.

"Hard to move fast when you've been in love with someone for years."

"Does she know?"

He shrugged. "I don't think so."

I'd suspected Jules had feelings for Sephy back when we'd been together, but I'd never been worried about it. This was *Julien.* I'd bet he had been beating himself up enough about liking his best friend's girl without me needing to pile on too.

"What am I supposed to do?"

"Apologise?" Jules stepped away and shrugged. "I don't know. This is between the two of you."

"Great," I mumbled and he squeezed my shoulder as he walked past. So I had to somehow convince the girl I'd loved and stupidly let go that she should give me a shot. How? Why?

I sighed. I needed to do more than just grovel. I needed to somehow show her that I was sorry. I needed to prove that I wasn't going to leave her again. Not ever, if she'd have me.

I'd spoken to Noel in our team building exercise that morning and we were going for drinks tonight. I had been relieved, mostly because with everything happening between me, Julien and Drew last night, I needed desperately to talk to someone. The alcohol was necessary, because I wasn't sure what she would say. I mean, I barely knew her and I was going to tell her I'd had a threesome with my boss. Technically, her boss too.

The session that morning had been tense as well. I'd been working in a group with people I'd never met before and we'd had to pitch a project to Noel as part of a pretend competition. The work had been fine. But Drew, Julien, and even Seth, had stopped by my table one-by-one, smiling and chatting—well, maybe flirting was a better descriptor, and other people had *definitely* noticed. Worse, Eileen was only a few doors down from me and ever since I'd spent the night with Julien she'd been watching me especially closely. It was annoying, but also worrying.

I probably shouldn't care, but I did. My reputation mattered, not only professionally but personally, and I could see the side-eyes directed my way. So when Noel sat down next to me at the bar, I was eager to get someone else's opinion on whether I'd made a giant mistake and also speculate about Seth's random change in behaviour. Was he jealous about what was going on with Julien and Drew? Ugh, men were so fickle.

Noel stared at me, her mouth parted as she tried to take in the information I'd just dumped on her. She reached for her drink and took a thoughtful sip before looking at me like she was going to say something, shaking her head, and having another sip.

"Well, whatever I thought you were going to say… it wasn't that."

I grimaced. "So you do think I've made a huge mistake."

"No." Noel took another small sip of her cocktail before she eyed me seriously. "It would have been a mistake for you not to do it. I mean, who wouldn't? Julien is hot. Like, in a major way."

I snorted. "He's also my boss."

"For now." She pointed out and I nodded slowly, watching our reflections in the mirror behind the bar. There were no fewer than three christmas trees in the room and the glittery red baubles winked at us in the reflection, I had to imagine it would be a dizzying display if you'd had a few drinks.

"He's Seth's best friend," I countered and she toasted me with her glass, careful not to slosh any liquid onto the hardwood bar top as she set it back down.

"And that's where you're going wrong."

"So I shouldn't have done it?"

"No, you shouldn't have done it without Seth."

I choked on my drink and Noel thumped me on the back. "You–You think I need to add more dicks into this equation?"

Noel laughed. "I mean, that's not exactly how I was going to phrase it, but yeah. You feel guilty because you're sleeping with your ex's besties, but I saw the way Seth was fawning over you this morning. He wants you just as much as they do."

He had been acting oddly, but that didn't mean he wanted to share me with the other two. Maybe he was just being friendly. "I don't know… Things between us are already complicated, I don't want to make them worse."

"I don't see how letting him join in would make things worse."

My cheeks flushed. "I can't believe I'm talking to you about this."

"Me either." She grinned, flashing the gap between her teeth. "But I'm not sorry about it."

I laughed with her and we ordered another round of drinks. A different bartender was working to the one we'd had last time but Noel flirted with him all the same and I watched, bemused, as he handed us the drinks for free.

"You're good at this."

"Sweetie, you're doing it with two of the hottest guys I've ever laid eyes on – I think you're doing just fine too." Another laugh escaped me and she smiled, eyes warm. "Maybe you just need to give him a chance. I've seen him pining over you in every session, there's no way he's not interested."

I rubbed the bridge of my nose. "I don't know if *I'm* interested. He dropped me before like it was easy. I don't want to open myself up to that again."

"Okay," she said slowly, one finger tapping the side of her glass absently and I bit back a smile as I glimpsed the snowmen she had painted onto her nails. "But just because that's how it felt, doesn't mean that's how it was." I raised an eyebrow and she wrinkled her nose. "I just mean, don't assume, right? Maybe he's just an arse who wants what he can't have, or maybe he's an idiot who knows what he lost."

I considered her words for a moment as I sipped my drink. It was possible I'd put words in Seth's mouth that hadn't really been said, but actions spoke louder than anything else… and he'd left. "I'll think about it."

"Make him work for it," Noel said as she took another swallow of her martini. A wicked look came over her face and she smirked at me. "Make him beg for it."

Now that *was* an interesting prospect.

CHAPTER 11

Sephy

"Okay!" Noel clapped her hands to gather the attention of the group and we all looked to her patiently as she beamed. It should have been illegal to be that perky so early in the morning. "I've paired you all up for the next activity, so once I call your name please find your partner and wait for my next instructions."

Noel ran down the list of names and my eyes roamed over the group, somehow now that we were outside it felt like there were a lot more of us. I stomped my feet a little, trying to keep my legs from going numb as I slipped on my thick gloves, when Noel finally called my name.

"Sephy and… Seth."

I widened my eyes at her and she grinned broadly as Seth stepped up next to me. *Traitor* I mouthed at her and she winked.

"Okay, now you're all in your pairs, I'm going to

hand around the equipment you'll need for this challenge. You should have a whistle, a map, and a compass and don't forget to wear your team headband! If you're missing anything let me know before you head out onto the trail okay?"

We all let out a chorus of agreement and I kept my gaze focused straight ahead, ignoring the way I could feel Seth watching me.

"The rules are simple! You're only allowed to work with your partner and the first pair to find the clearing on your map will be the winners. If you get in trouble, blow your whistle and one of us will come and help you." She nodded to the resort staff who were milling around before smiling at us all again.

I hid a yawn as I looked over the map that had been passed around. Orienteering was not my strong suit, I could barely navigate the tube, let alone a forest. Seth lived for this kind of stuff though, it was almost like a treasure hunt. Sure enough, an excited smile was tugging at his mouth as he peered over my shoulder at the map.

"You should take the lead," I said quietly and handed the map over, swapping it for the whistle in his hand and then looking down distastefully at the reindeer headband we'd been given. I pressed the button on the side and the brown fuzzy antlers lit up. This had Noel written all over it. "I can try and navigate with the compass if you want."

"Sure," he said easily, fingertips barely brushing mine as he handed over the cold compass and slipped on his own light-up ears. "We've got this." His mouth was curled into a familiar smile, a little dimple popping in his cheek and I bit my lip as I fought off the swell of emotion that accompanied the sight of it.

Noel counted down and we all rushed off into the snowy pines as soon as she said go, hunting for the best trail to take us to the clearing first. Seth was frowning down at our map as we hovered next to a huge tree.

"Which way?"

His eyebrows furrowed as he turned the map slightly before nodding to himself. "Let's carry on straight for now."

"Sure," I murmured, half-wanting to get this over with and half-curious as to where this might go. Thanks to Noel's meddling, we now had plenty of time together on our own to talk. Or other things. *No, it's way too cold for that.* And I shouldn't have been thinking about *other things* anyway. I loved Seth, that didn't mean I should let him back into my life again.

It was surprisingly sunny out, considering how chilly it was, and my boots made large divots in the snow as we plodded on. This trail was normally used as part of the wildlife tour, I wasn't really sure what constituted as *wildlife* but I was just hoping it didn't include bears.

We rounded a corner and came to an abrupt dead-end where a river ran. I couldn't imagine Noel wanted us to wade across, so I turned back to Seth with a raised eyebrow. "Did we take a wrong turn?"

"Must have." He cleared his throat and peered

down at the map again, tapping his foot impatiently and sending small puffs of snow up into the air. "Let's head that way," he said, pointing off to the right where a small trail barely showed through the trees.

"Are you sure? I don't see any footprints, nobody else came through here."

"It's a shortcut."

I eyed him doubtfully but followed when he pushed a low-hanging branch aside for me. The trail was narrow, just about enough room for one large person walking single file, with only more trees on either side of us and my stupid antlers kept getting caught on foliage. Icicles hung down off of the branches and shone in the sunlight and despite the early start, and the company, I had to admit it was very beautiful out here.

We couldn't have been walking for any longer than ten minutes before Seth stopped so abruptly I walked into his back. He steadied me before I could fall and I peered around him to see another dead end.

"A shortcut, huh?"

"The map must be wrong."

"Or maybe you just can't read it."

Seth frowned. "I didn't read it wrong."

"Oh, so the two dead ends were just a coincidence."

He shrugged. "Must be."

I bit back a growl as he watched me, blinking innocently. Was he trying deliberately to piss me off?

"Why can't you ever admit that you're wrong?" I

demanded, stepping a little closer and folding my arms across my chest when his eyes dropped to my mouth. "Stop that."

He jerked them back up again. "If I was wrong, I'd admit it."

"Then what do you call this, right now!" I threw my hands up as I gestured around us, stepping close and poking a finger into his chest.

"Unlucky?"

"You are so—" I huffed out a breath. "You haven't changed at all."

The amused look in his eyes dropped away and he frowned. "No, I haven't."

He didn't regret it then, for all his flirtation now that he was here, he didn't regret walking out of that door and leaving me behind. I shook my head, blinking back the stupid fucking tears that had appeared in my eyes out of nowhere as I spun around to walk away. Seth's hand caught mine and he tugged me back to face him.

"I haven't changed," he said earnestly, like it made it any better when he said it the second time around, like it would hurt less. "I still drink two cups of coffee in the morning before work and I still sing *Kansas* in the shower and I am still," he said moving closer, his eyes watching mine with an intensity that made my mouth go dry, "the guy that's so in love with you it hurts. None of that's changed."

I swallowed hard. "You're still the guy who walked away. Who left me. Who—"

"I shouldn't have!" His voice echoed strangely, blanketed by the snow and caught in the fir trees and the words knocked around in my head over and over until I knew I would be hearing them in my dreams.

"But you did," I said quietly. "How am I supposed to trust you? How am I supposed to forget that?" Snow started falling heavier around us and I blinked it out of my eyes as it fell in Seth's hair, caught in his lashes.

"You don't have to forget," he said quietly, stepping a little closer as his hand came up between us to cup my jaw and then a tiny smirk formed on his mouth. "You just have to tell me you don't still want this."

He kissed me. One second my tongue was wrapped around a swear word, the next it was curled around his. He tasted the same as he always did, like spearmint, and his mouth was cold as it nipped at mine. My hand curled into his coat, tugging him closer and his lips hungrily devoured every gasp I made as we kissed. The tree branches pressed into my back, snow bouncing off their leaves and showering us with ice, but Seth's hands were on my cheeks and mine were locked around his neck and I didn't know if I would be able to let go again.

Seth broke the kiss and I stumbled away a step and out of his arms, my eyes wide. "What are we doing? You cant—I can't—"

He kissed me again and I mumbled against his lips for a second before I sank into it, sucking on his lower lip and then backing away when he moaned.

"Stop that! We shouldn't be doing this. *You* walked away, not me."

"You could have followed me."

"You know I needed to be here."

"I needed to be wherever you were," he admitted.

I stared at him. "You didn't read the map wrong at all, did you?"

A blush seared across his cheeks but he met my eyes with a hint of defiance. "I told you, I wasn't wrong."

"There are easier ways to get me alone than getting us lost in the woods."

Seth sighed and reached for my hand but I yanked it away. "We're not lost. And I wouldn't have resorted to cornering you if you hadn't been avoiding me."

I sniffed, spinning back the way we'd come. "I haven't been avoiding you—"

"Sephy, look out!"

Something hard landed on me and it took a second for me to realise it was Seth.

"What the hell is wrong with you?" I demanded and nudged him, trying to get up. He didn't move. "Seth?"

He groaned and I put my hand on his shoulder tentatively before he rolled himself off me. "Ouch."

"What happened?"

He raised a wobbly hand in the air and pointed vaguely at the large tree we'd just walked under. "Branch."

I followed his hand and realised a large icicle-clad

branch was now on the floor where we had been standing. It looked heavy enough that if it had got me on the head I probably would have been knocked out or—

My eyes shot back to Seth and I screamed when I saw the thin line of blood trickling down his face. "Oh my god." I wasn't good with blood, *at all.* I fumbled for the whistle I had stowed in my coat pocket and had to lick my lips and swallow twice before I could get any noise out of it.

"S'just a scratch," Seth slurred and I gently pushed him back to the snowy floor when he tried to stand up, his light up antlers flickering on the ground.

"You could have a concussion!"

I blew on the whistle again and two of the resort rangers ambled around the corner, eyes widening when they saw Seth on the floor. I pointed at the branch as they jogged the rest of the way over and shakily explained what had happened, biting back tears as they checked Seth's head wound.

Thankfully it had stopped bleeding and after the initial shock wore off, he seemed fine, if a little sore. I was also feeling a little cold and stiff after being tackled to the ground, but I couldn't complain too much considering he'd taken a head injury for me.

"Don't think this means everything is suddenly forgiven between us," I warned him as I helped him back to the lodge. "Thank you," I said a little more quietly and he smiled at me.

"Anytime, love."

Juilen swung open their front door dressed in a suit, either getting ready to leave for a meeting or just got back. He looked between us with his face unreadable and I bit my lip, worried he might be mad to see me with Seth.

"What happened?" he said once he noticed the cut on Seth's head.

"A branch fell on his head," I said dryly as we made it to the door. Drew appeared behind Julien, glancing between the three of us before waggling his eyebrows at me and I shot him a mock glare.

"Are you going to kiss it better for him?" Drew teased, pouting at me.

"She already did," Seth said smugly and I could feel myself turning red as I glared at him. Neither Jules or Drew looked upset by the admission though, if anything Julien looked… pleased?

"Good." Drew winked as we peeled off our snow-wet coats and shoes. "I hate it when Mom and Dad fight."

"Drew," I sighed tiredly and he immediately quit his joking, walking over and wrapping his arms around my waist from behind.

Julien pressed a kiss to my cheek before checking on Seth's head. "How about a massage?"

There was no getting anything by Jules, he'd obviously noticed me wincing as I moved and I smiled gratefully.

"How generous of you to offer," Seth said dryly and Julien waved him off. Drew pulled away, heading to the kitchen, as Julien steered me to the sofa. He grabbed a cushion and set it on the floor for me and then ran his fingers along my back and shoulder, searching for knots. I groaned when he found a particularly sore spot and his hands paused for a second.

"Sorry," I murmured and he chuckled.

"You don't need to be. I'm just trying to keep myself in check."

"You don't have to," I mimicked and he laughed, the soothing rumble making me feel cosy as it echoed through my chest.

"I don't think Seth is up for it right now, darling, and it would be rude of us not to invite him again," he said knowingly. I kept quiet, not sure what my thoughts on the matter were, even though deep down I suspected I already had my answer. But just because I loved Seth, didn't mean I could forgive him.

"Here you go," Drew said cheerfully as he deposited a warm mug of hot chocolate in my hands. "I'm going to check on Seth," he said, nodding upstairs where Seth had gone to lie down.

I thanked him and took a sip, nearly choking. "Drew, is there brandy in this?"

He grinned at me, already half-way up the stairs. "You looked like you needed it."

He was right, so I just rolled my eyes as I sipped, enjoying the feeling of Jules' hands running over my body as I relaxed.

"You two kissed," Jules said, clearly deciding not to beat around the bush any longer.

"It was a mistake," I said firmly, unsure if I was trying to convince him or myself.

"Did you enjoy it?

I didn't answer and Jules laughed quietly.

"It's okay to forgive him, you know. He made a mistake."

"Actions have consequences," I said stiffly and Jules hummed in agreement.

"If you want him too, then the only person you're hurting by not forgiving him is yourself."

I frowned, not liking the logic of his words and shivered as a drop of icy water fell from my damp hair. "Ugh melted snow." It wasn't an elegant change of subject, but I was hoping he'd get the hint and drop it, for now at least.

"Come on," Julien said, tugging on the end of my hair.

"Where are we going?"

"You need a bath."

I perked up a little. "Are you going to help me wash?"

I couldn't be sure, but it looked like he blushed. "I'd love to."

We started up the stairs and I looked around with interest as we came to the landing, I'd been a little too distracted to take anything in the last time I'd been up here. Drew stuck his head out of a room just ahead and looked at us. "Did I hear something about a bath?"

I laughed. "You can come too if you like." I leaned against the wall with Drew as Julien strode on to what I assumed was the bathroom and got the bath running.

"Need extra hands, love? You must be especially filthy."

My throat went dry and I peered in through the door Drew was leaning against and realised it was Seth's room. I pushed down my lust and annoyance – bastard knew I loved it when he called me that.

"I don't remember inviting you," I said cooly and Drew looked between us like he was settling into a particularly good show.

"And here I was, all ready for a bath," he said slyly and I realised why when I looked through the doorway and found him clad in only a towel. I worked hard to keep my breathing even, to stop my eyes from sliding down his abs or lower. "I called dibs, love."

Seth stepped forward and Drew stayed where he was, smirking as he watched me struggle.

The warmth of his bare skin invaded my senses and my eyes dropped down to his lips. "Maybe we can share," I said breathily and a slow smile curled Seth's mouth. I mentally shook myself, annoyed I'd succumbed so easily. "How's your head?"

"Never had any complaints," he said smoothly and I gaped.

"Bath's nearly ready," Julien called and I had never been so grateful for an interruption before.

"Coming!" I called and Drew smirked, opening his mouth. I pressed a finger to his lips. "Don't even say it." He shook with silent laughter as I huffed and stalked off to the bathroom.

It smelled incredible in there, like he'd dumped an entire bottle of bubble bath into the water. Steam floated up into the air and I relaxed as the warmth seeped into me. Seth strode into the room and didn't even look at me before he dropped his towel and stepped gingerly into the water. We would have no problem both fitting, thankfully. The thing was so big it put the copper tub in my hotel room to shame.

Drew wandered in too and kissed me on the cheek. "Do you want some help, gorgeous?"

I nodded and he tugged up the jumper I was wearing, pulling it over my head easily before he brushed my hair flat again. Julien stroked his hands over my shoulders and when Drew undid the clasp on my bra, Jules pushed down the straps, bearing my breasts. Seth watched from the tub, sprawled lazily against the wall, his blue eyes dark as Drew pushed down the hot pink joggers I was wearing, followed by my leggings.

"Fuck woman, how many layers are you wearing?"

"It's cold outside," I said defensively and Drew chuckled as he hooked his fingers around my thong and tugged.

I stepped toward the bath and paused when Drew's arm around my waist pulled me to a stop.

"Don't I deserve a kiss for being so helpful?"

I smirked, leaning forward and kissing him on the cheek and then squealing when Julien grabbed me and pulled me back to them, capturing my mouth in a blazing kiss that absolutely melted me before tilting my head for Drew. His kiss was just as hot, his tongue stroking mine in a way that reminded me of just how talented he'd been with it between my legs. He grinned when he pulled away, like he'd done it deliberately. He probably had.

I stepped into the hot water and groaned. It was the perfect temperature, near scalding, but it worked to loosen the muscles that were still sore. I sighed, my eyes falling closed as I leaned against the side of the bath. The water sloshed gently and then two sets of soapy hands worked along my shoulders, breasts, stomach and back, massaging gently and then rinsing me free of suds.

"Come on, love. I've got you." Seth's hands guided me back as he lay my head back in the water, combing his fingers through the wind-knots in my hair and then propping me up against his chest as he shampooed my head, massaging my scalp until I turned to putty against him. I heard Drew chuckle and my eyes flew open, finding him instantly. He and Jules sat on the floor, arms wet up to their elbows from where they'd washed me, and their eyes were intent on us.

Seth washed the shampoo free before adding some floral smelling conditioner to my wet strands and working it through.

"I'm sorry," he murmured in my ear, his voice

sending goosebumps over my skin. "I promise I won't ever let you down again and I will prove it to you every damn day, Sephy."

It felt like my heart beat unevenly at his words. They were everything I wanted to hear, and yet part of me didn't trust them. Not yet.

"Trust is earned," I said quietly and he nodded.

"I know. I'm only asking that you give me a chance to earn it."

I considered that, my eyes finding Jules' as I chewed on Seth's words. Jules' head inclined slightly, he wanted me to give Seth a shot.

Seth rinsed the conditioner out, the warm water feeling somehow sensual as his fingers combed through my hair and stroked along my neck. He was careful to keep it out of my eyes as he worked and I stared up at him, taking in the strong lines of his face as he concentrated.

When he was done, he met my gaze and I didn't shy away.

"You've got a lot more grovelling to do," I warned and he smirked.

"I've never been afraid to get down on my knees, love."

I bit back my smile but I knew he'd seen my lips twitch. Seth pulled me away from his chest, propping me up against the back of the bath and I frowned. "What are you doing?"

"Getting a head start on my grovelling." He shot Drew and Jules a speculative eyebrow tilt and I looked back and forth between them, wondering what it meant. "I bet I can make you come before I run out of air."

I didn't get a chance to reply before he sank beneath the surface. My legs instinctively opened wide for him and I gasped at the first touch of his tongue against my clit. Drew gave a happy sigh as he watched me squirm.

"Didn't get to see you last time, what with my face being buried between your legs and all, but damn, gorgeous. You're so fucking hot."

Jules smiled and I tried to smile back but got distracted when Seth sucked on my clit and plunged his tongue into me. How long could he realistically hold his breath for? No wonder he wasn't holding back.

"Shall we offer an assist?" Jules asked Drew, who smirked in response.

"It would be rude not to," he replied, shifting forward to cup one of my breasts in his hand before bending forward and sucking the nipple into his mouth, teasing me with his tongue. "Not when you're spread out for us like the most delicious meal I've ever seen."

Julien kissed me before I could reply and I moaned into his mouth as Seth fucked me with his tongue relentlessly. My hips bucked and Drew switched to my other breast, rolling the nipple of the other between his fingers and sending electricity pulsing through me.

I panted into Julien's mouth, my eyes locked on his as he watched me.

"You are so beautiful," he whispered. One finger slid into me and my cries echoed through the bathroom as I approached the edge. "Come for us, Sephy. Now."

I couldn't hold back, my pussy clenching around Seth's finger and pulsing around his tongue as I orgasmed and he surfaced a moment later, panting but looking smug.

Jules pressed a kiss to my forehead and reached for a fluffy white towel hanging on the radiator. "Come on," he said, holding it open for me.

I reached for him, trying not to slip in the water we'd splashed everywhere, and shivered a little until it was wrapped around me. It was still warm from the rad and Jules smoothed his hand up and down it soothingly. I wasn't sure I'd ever felt more sated, cared for, or relaxed.

Drew threw another towel over my head and scooped my hair out of the other towel, somehow wrapping it expertly so that my hair stopped dripping on my face, and then chucked another towel to Seth as he came out of the bath. The white towel tented around his cock but he shook his head when he saw me notice.

"Grovelling, remember?"

I smiled slightly as Julien continued to rub soothing circles into my back and Drew rubbed my arse before leading me out of the bathroom to bed.

CHAPTER 12
Drew

"What do you want to drink?" Sephy smiled up at me from her place at the bar and I pulled my eyes away from the cleavage that was practically spilling out of the front of her silky pink dress. It wasn't that it was inappropriate, she was just that stunning, and the silky material emphasised her every curve while catching the light and—

"Drew?" she said, a smile curving her full bottom lip and I laughed.

"Sorry, I'll just have a beer please."

The bartender read out what they had on tap and I tuned her out, letting Sephy choose for me. I wasn't a big drinker really, when she'd suggested we get a drink after dinner I'd agreed simply because I wanted to spend time with her.

"Thanks." I took a sip as the glass was set down and then blew out a big breath. "I think that burger might have killed me if I'd finished it. Did you see the size of that thing?"

Sephy laughed and nodded, humouring me. Probably because I'd exclaimed that exact same thing about three times while I'd been devouring it.

"How was your chicken thing?"

"It was alright." She grinned. "Not as big as your burger."

One of the things I liked most about Sephy was that when she teased me, which was often, her blue eyes seemed to get lighter. It was like up until that moment she'd been carrying the weight of the world and managed to forget it for a few moments to laugh with me.

Last night had felt like maybe one of the best of my life, seeing this gorgeous woman who so often had her guards up completely relax had given me more pleasure than I'd been expecting. "How do you feel after last night?" Sephy had pretty much passed out in Jules' bed after the wet 'n' wild bath we'd all shared and I knew she had a tendency to overthink things, it made me worried about what had been brewing in that mind of hers since she'd left the lodge this morning.

"Happy," she said, surprising me. "You look shocked."

I grinned. "That's because I'm terrible at hiding my emotions or repressing my thoughts."

"You do have a serious lack of filter." My smile dimmed slightly, unsure if that was a good thing, until she continued, "It's one of the things I like most about you. I never have to guess what you're thinking or if something's wrong, because you'll just tell me."

"Of course," I said, confused and she pressed a sweet kiss to my cheek.

"Clearly you don't understand how rare that is in a man. Or anyone, really."

I shrugged. "It's not an approach everyone has liked."

She sipped her drink, watching me as she swallowed and for some reason *that* was what had my dick standing to attention.

"Then those people are idiots." She smirked. "But it's to my benefit really, now I get you all to myself."

"Oh?" I asked as she blushed. "You're sealing the deal with me already, are you? We're official?"

She played with the straw in the tall glass of her cocktail, pursing her lips as she considered her response. "Is that… okay? I mean, with all of you? I like you, Drew, but—"

"It's better when we're all together," I finished for her and she looked relieved as she nodded.

"Exactly. I'm not sure where things stand with me and Seth right now, I'm definitely not through making him grovel." She smiled wickedly and I laughed, approving of the mix of lust and vengeance that was on her face. "But I'm willing to try."

"That's all that matters," I said seriously and she smiled.

"Are you going to go skiing while you're here?"

I wrinkled my nose. "Maybe, I don't know. It's only

fun if Jules comes too, he's the best out of all of us so he's the most fun to race down the slopes."

Sephy nodded. "I've never been skiing before."

I perked up. "I can teach you if you like."

She grimaced. "I'm not sure I'd enjoy it to be honest, I'd much rather watch you guys ski while I sit in the warm with a hot chocolate."

"Can't fault you there." I tilted my beer at her in a salute as I took a drink.

"Let's play a game." Sephy grinned and I raised my eyebrows in amusement at the excitement in her voice.

"Why?"

"Because I want to get to know you better."

"Oh, I don't know," I whispered, leaning in close to her ear. "I think we've got to know each other pretty well already."

She rolled her eyes. "Let's play two truths and a lie."

I chuckled, gesturing that she should go first. She waited until the bartender brought her over a soda before saying anything. There was a mischief in her eyes that was seriously turning me on, I liked seeing her like this. Happy.

"Okay. I once got stuck on a broken down tube for an hour. I've never done anal. My favourite colour is purple."

I snorted at her choices and she raised her eyebrows at me in response. "So I need to pick out the lie?"

"Yep."

I watched her sip on her lemonade as I thought it over. The tube was ancient, so it didn't seem impossible that she'd been stuck on one. Anal… I don't know. Sephy seemed open, but that didn't mean she'd done it before. Something about her seemed… inexperienced. Hesitant. But maybe that was just lack of confidence. As for the colour… well, it could definitely be purple, she seemed to love wearing an abundance of colour in general.

"Anal," I decided and her lips drew up into a smirk.

"My favourite colour is pink."

I choked on my sip of beer, loving the flirty way she leaned closer to me, her fingers curling around my arm like we were sharing secrets. I guessed in a way, we were.

"Your turn," she said primly and I chuckled.

"Hmm, let me think. I was once an extra on a medical drama. I'm an excellent singer. My fiancé cheated on me with her personal trainer after trying to steal my money."

Sephy's mouth popped open at the last comment and I felt an odd swooping sensation in my stomach. I didn't really like to talk about what had happened with Bethany, but it wasn't because I still loved her or anything like that. I just felt… ashamed. Stupid. How could I have missed that my fiancé hadn't really known me at all? Hadn't even cared to try? I'd been blinded by my parents' approval and the pretty picture we'd made, but a relationship needed to be more than that, as I now knew. I hadn't spoken to my parents for months now, and it was probably wrong for me to place so much of the blame on them, but it was easier to be mad at them than at myself.

I watched Sephy bite her lip as she considered my truths and a lie. *Because I want to get to know you better.* Would she shy away from the truth I'd given her? Pretend ignorance? Or would she face it head on with me?

"You weren't on a medical drama," she said at last and I smiled.

"I'm a terrible singer."

"I'm sorry about your fiancé, that's terrible." Her hand covered mine as she leaned in and pressed a kiss to my cheek.

"It's okay, maybe next time I'll get it right," I murmured softly and the blush that rose to her cheeks brought me an absurd amount of pleasure.

"So you really were an extra?"

I grinned. "I was obsessed with *Grey's Anatomy* and my dad knew one of the producers."

She laughed with me and we chattered on as we finished our drinks. It was maybe the most pleasant, comfortable date I'd ever been on. Sephy stood and I reached for my wallet, pausing when she scrunched her eyebrows together. "What are you doing?"

"I was going to pay our restaurant tab?"

She shook her head, patting my cheek. "You're such a loveable idiot. Did you think they'd let us wander around here if we hadn't already paid?"

I blinked at her, stunned. "You mean, you paid for dinner?"

"When you were in the bathroom," she confirmed and then laughed. "I do have my own money, you know."

I don't know why that hit me so hard, but it did. I shoved my hands in my pockets so she wouldn't see them shake, but I'd never been good at hiding my emotions and Sephy's face softened as she watched me. She stepped close, the sweetness of her perfume soothing my senses as she pressed her mouth to mine, coaxing me into a slow kiss that made me crave more.

Her cheeks were flushed and she seemed a little breathless when she pulled away. "Do you fancy a walk in the snow?"

I looked down at her heels doubtfully. "Tell me you at least have a coat."

She laughed and grabbed it from her chair, shrugging it on. "I guess you'll just have to hold me tight to make sure I don't fall over."

I didn't have a single problem with that and her grin widened.

"Thank you for dinner," I said quietly in her ear as we passed through the bar and into the lobby.

"Anytime." She kissed me again, and I believed her.

We both shivered as we stepped out into the cool night air and I tucked Sephy in close to my side. The snow had eased, though I was sure it would start coming down again at some point. There was barely any wind though, which was nice because normally it was so cold it would cut right through you. It felt like we were in our own winter wonderland, the night still, the lights that lit the pathway to the lodges sending a warm glow over our faces as we walked and the errant sound of chatter from the hotel faded as we got further away. It was nice to not think about anything other than Sephy's hand in mine.

Suddenly, she lurched to the side and I gasped, thinking she'd fallen, only to rear back as something cold hit me in the middle of my forehead, exploding into a powdery puff. Sephy's laughter rang out around us as I gaped at her before lunging into action, scooping my own handful of snow and launching it back at her.

She shrieked as she dodged and I caught her before she could fall. Her fingers were now as cold as my own and I pressed a kiss to their tips, nipping one playfully and making her breath catch. Desire darkened her eyes to a deep blue and our laughter faded away, replaced by an entirely different emotion.

We reached for each other at the same time and our lips met in a feverish kiss, hungry in a way I'd never experienced before, and the more I made her moan, the more I wanted her.

"Sephy," I mumbled against her and felt her smile.

"I have something for you," she said and I couldn't fathom what else she could give me when she'd already given more than I could have asked for – herself.

She wrapped her hand around mine and tugged

me off of the pathway, to the very edge of the woods and I looked around warily. It may have helped fix things between Seth and Sephy, but I didn't fancy taking a heroic blow to my head right that second.

"What are we doing?" I had my answer a second later though when she kissed me hard, biting my lower lip, and I sighed in pleasure as her hands ran through my hair, tugging lightly. I was unprepared, however, for her to drop to her knees in the snow.

"You'll get cold," I protested as she reached for my dick, stroking me through my trousers, and I groaned as my eyes fell shut. "No fair."

She laughed breathlessly and I clenched my jaw as I forced myself to think clearly.

"You don't need to do this, Sephy. I don't want you to get—"

"Shh," she said as she lowered the zipper and reached inside to feel me. "Do you want this?"

I swallowed. "Yes, but—"

Her mouth wrapped around my head and I was hypnotised as I watched her, lost in the feel of her tongue against me. She pulled back and the cold air nipped at my skin, making me wince. "Don't worry," she murmured, "I'll keep you warm."

She was true to her word, swallowing me down almost to my base and looking up at me from the ground, her big blue eyes like beacons. So. Fucking. Gorgeous.

The low hum in her throat made me gasp her name and she smirked as she pulled back, focusing her mouth and tongue on my head until she took me in again. It felt like the stars above our heads were swimming, or maybe I was just dizzy as all the blood in my body rushed to my dick.

"Sephy—" I called warningly, choking when she increased her pace and my dick hit the back of her throat. I came so hard I wasn't sure if I had blacked out for a second. Sephy licked her lips and tucked me away before she stood and kissed me on the cheek.

"That's better." Her voice was a satisfied purr and I let her walk me to the lodge in a daze. Best. Date. Ever.

"Are you coming inside?" I said to her as we approached the door, still somewhat dizzy.

"If that's okay." Her smile was sweet as she pulled her arm out of mine. "Seth promised to show me the sauna."

"Of course." I stopped her before we opened the door, cupping her face in my palm as our breath fogged in the cold air. "Thank you. For everything."

Sephy tilted her chin and I pressed my lips to hers in a slow kiss, we pulled apart reluctantly and I stroked her cheek before reaching behind her to let us inside.

Julien looked up from the sofa as we kicked off our shoes and Sephy grinned at him, walking over to give him a kiss of his own before she called out to Seth and made her way upstairs. I stood in the foyer for a second, just watching her move, before Jules called my name and I blinked dumbly at him.

"Everything okay?"

I walked over and collapsed next to him on the

couch. "I—" I shook my head. It was crazy how something so small had wracked me so thoroughly but when you had money, that was usually all anybody saw. It definitely affected how they treated you. But not with Sephy.

"What is it?" Jules placed a hand on my shoulder as he peered into my face and I took a deep breath, letting it out in a rush until my head felt slightly clearer.

"She paid for dinner."

"Okay?" Julien raised one eyebrow and I bit my lip as I stood and paced in front of the fireplace, letting it warm my legs. "Is that a bad thing?"

"I don't think a woman has ever bought me dinner before."

"Never?"

"Never," I confirmed and Julien sat back against the sofa, not saying anything more and just letting me work it out. "How long does it take to fall in love?"

He shrugged. "It's different for everyone. You loved your ex, right?"

I'd definitely thought so at the time, but now… "It's not the same."

"As?"

"As Sephy."

The fireplace crackled as Julien stood and offered me the drink he'd clearly poured for himself and had on the small table by his side. "Congrats, you're in love."

"Isn't it too soon?" I sipped the drink and looked

down at it in surprise. It was sweet and creamy but still burned like alcohol. "What is this?"

"*Baileys.* And you don't have to say anything to her yet, give it time."

"Time," I said, taking another sip and nodding. "This is good."

"Occasionally us Brits do something right." Julien took the glass from me and drank before handing it back.

"I think I love her." I stared out of the window, watching the snow drift by lazily and Jules joined me, nodding slowly.

"Yeah, me too."

"She gave me a blow job in the woods."

Julien snorted. "I'm surprised your dick didn't fall off from the cold."

"I was concerned about that," I admitted.

Sephy squealed upstairs and Seth's low chuckle followed her as she appeared on the landing and peered down at us before walking down the first set of stairs and pausing at the top of the next. "We're going down to the sauna, aren't you coming?"

I smiled. "Lead the way, gorgeous."

CHAPTER 13

Sephy

I really didn't know why some companies insisted on making such long, cheesy, and cheap training videos. They usually came complete with a dull message from a CEO or head of whatever department they were touting in the video, this was the second one we'd watched as part of this session and even Noel's cheer had faded as the third one rolled around.

I wished I could say I was paying attention. But that was difficult, given that I was seated next to Julien. He was supposed to be giving us some speech at the end of the corporate movie marathon, and I planned on getting him to look over my own presentation that I had to deliver in the final stakeholder meeting of the conference in just over a week's time. I was proud of the initiative I'd put into place for the entry level recruitment – it had taken lots of long hours and blood, sweat, and tears to pull off. I had to make sure I didn't sell it, or myself, short in the meeting.

Jules' hand found my leg beneath the table and squeezed lightly, as if he could tell that I was stressing instead of listening to Debbie from compliance drone on about the importance of GDPR practices and locking your laptop when you leave your desk. Apparently there was going to be an interactive quiz at the end, which managed to sound more like a threat to pay attention thananything else. Luckily, these things were all common sense: *don't click the suspicious link that Joan sent you at one in the morning, don't give out your password* – why they felt we needed a two-hour session on this, I'd never understand.

Jules nudged me and I jolted, realising I'd been moments away from nodding off. He looked like he was fighting a smile, and his eyes were warm as he turned to me. For a second, it felt like we were lost just staring at each other. His eyes flicked to my mouth and I bit my lip. Knowing I couldn't kiss him right here, right now, somehow made me want it more. That probably spoke to some deep psychological issues, or maybe it was just human nature, all I knew was that I'd never wanted Julien more than I did in that moment.

The air between us was so electric I was surprised the hair on my arms wasn't standing up. A muscle in his sharp jaw ticked as he looked away from me.

"You need to stop looking at me like that, darling." His voice was low, meant for my ears alone, and there was something infinitely sexy about being alone in a room full of people. Like we had a secret nobody else knew.

I shifted restlessly as my underwear started to cling to me uncomfortably and the shadow of a smirk crossed Jules' face as he noted the movement. His hand dropped to my leg again and I stilled as he pressed little, tortuous circles into my knee.

He was taunting me deliberately, the bastard.

The video ended and I jumped when Julien stood up next to me, buttoning his suit jacket closed and covering the bulge that had appeared in his trousers. I looked up and caught Eileen's eye uncomfortably, had she been watching us? There was an odd expression on her face, like she was choking on something unpleasant, and I shifted my gaze away quickly to focus back on Julien. He strode to the front of the room and I knew I wasn't the only one who watched him as he walked, Jules had been blessed with an incredible butt and I flushed, remembering the feel of the muscles there clenching underneath my hands when he'd fucked me.

"Thanks for your time this morning guys, I hope we all found those clips useful." He didn't look in my direction, but I knew the amused tilt to his mouth was for me. "If you've got any questions, now's your chance to ask. Yes, Kelly?"

God, Jules was ridiculously sexy. I'd never understood the appeal of a man in charge before, but something in the way he held himself, the confidence in which he smoothly answered the questions made me tingle. Or maybe it was just how good he looked in a suit.

Julien smiled, joking easily with one of the guys on the marketing team. This was obviously the part of running the business that he enjoyed, talking to his employees – which was the polar opposite for me, of course. I'd much rather keep my head down and get on with things than chat with people by the coffee machine, for the most part anyway.

Jules headed back to his seat and Noel clapped a couple of times but gave up when nobody else joined in. "Great! Thanks so much for that quick Q&A, Julien. We've just got the quiz to do and then we'll wrap up for today."

Noel called up a couple of volunteers for each side of the room and decided to make a competition out of things. A low buzz of noise immediately started up and I relaxed, glad that I could shake off my sleepiness now that the room was looking alive again.

"You did great," I said to Jules when he sat down again. "How do you keep so calm facing a room full of people?"

"You find that hard?" I shrugged and he smiled slightly. "I never would have known."

"Thanks."

"You're nervous about your presentation, then?"

"A little." A lot.

"I can take a look at it later if you like? We can go over it together." His smile was sweet and his icy blue eyes made me melt as focused absolutely on me.

"That would be amazing, if you're sure you don't mind."

He tapped his chin, pretending to think. "Hmm, spend extra time with a beautiful girl, or go back to the lodge and listen to Drew going on about a trip in the woods he recently took..."

I knew my face was likely flaming red and Julien chuckled. It had been a bit spur of the moment and my legs had been freezing by the time I was done, but I'd just wanted to make sure Drew knew that someone cared about him. That *I* cared.

"What exactly did he say?"

"Honestly, not much. I think you broke him because he was kind of dazed all night. Not in a bad way," Julien reassured. "More like he was... awed."

"He did seem pretty surprised that I paid for dinner," I admitted and Jules' eyebrows rose.

"I don't think anyone's ever bought Drew dinner in his life." Jules laughed a little but I thought that was kind of sad. Just because Drew had money didn't mean things shouldn't be equal in a relationship, or as equal as was possible anyway.

"It was a small thing." I shrugged. "It made me sad that he was so blown away by it. He deserved better."

"He told you about Bethany?"

"We didn't have a huge discussion about it or anything, it was more in passing."

Jules nodded thoughtfully. "He hardly ever talks about her."

I sniffed. "Sounds like there's not much to say."

His lip twitched and I looked back to the front of the room to avoid his probing gaze.

"Sephy, are you jealous?"

I scoffed. "Why would I be jealous?"

"Well, Drew did happen to mention something else about you guys being official—"

"All of us," I cut in and then held my breath, nervously waiting for his reaction. Julien didn't even bat an eyelid as he nodded.

"Yes, all of us. So I guess it just coincidentally seemed like you were getting defensive over him—"

"I just think he deserves good things!" I said, somewhat shrilly and Jules snorted.

"Are you going to let me finish a sentence?"

"Just did," I challenged and something flashed in his eyes that made my breasts tingle as sensation ran through my body like a live wire. "What is it, Jules? Are you jealous that I'm jealous?"

He laughed, breaking the tension somewhat but heat still simmered in his gaze when he looked at me. "Not at all, it's hot."

I smiled slightly. I liked the fact that there wasn't tension between us in our little group. I didn't think I could be with only one of them without the other two, regardless of what Seth and I had once shared. Maybe I was getting ahead of myself, but I'd known Julien and Seth for a long time, and even though I'd only just found Drew, things between us felt as easy as breathing.

The quiz ended and a loud cheer went up on the other side of the room, who had apparently won the quiz. Noel smiled indulgently, clapping along with everyone else and shooting me a wink when she saw how close I was sitting to Julien. I probably had a few things to fill her in on, namely that I'd taken her advice when it came to Seth and, so far, I didn't regret it.

Chairs scraped back as people got to their feet and I followed suit, pausing only when Jules placed a hand on my arm. The conference room quickly emptied until we were the last people in there.

"What's up?"

"Nothing," he said, a wickedness curling his mouth. "Nothing at all."

He kissed me and I whimpered in relief, had been craving him the whole session and was finally now getting a taste. It was like I'd been edging and Julien was the one finally bringing the pleasure. He nipped at my lip and I moaned, breathing hard when he reached down and lifted me onto the table, my legs making a cage around his as we pressed our bodies together.

He was already hard for me and I smirked as I ran a finger teasingly over him through his trousers. He snatched my hand away and kissed the spot just beneath my ear that he knew drove me crazy, I arched up, craving more of him, needing him, and he obliged.

The sound of the door opening made us both freeze and I peeked over his shoulder with wide eyes before grimacing. Fuck.

"Oh! I'm sorry. I didn't think anyone would be in here." Eileen. Of course it was Eileen. Because why would a nice, quiet person who wasn't known as the office gossip be the one to find me kissing the boss? "I, um, just forgot my coat." She pointed vaguely off to the side but didn't move. Was she just going to stand there? Should we say something?

God, she was going to tell everyone. My presentation was ruined before it had even started if this got back to the board and department heads.

"Well, I'll be on my way," she said, grabbing the coat she'd apparently forgotten and bustling over to the door, her short brown hair swaying with her steps as she turned to look back at us, her glasses glinting in the lights.

The door closed softly behind her but it felt like a bomb had just been dropped in our lap.

"What are we going to do?"

Julien rested his forehead against mine. "Nothing."

"You do realise who that was, right?"

"Yes."

"And you're okay with everyone in the bloody company knowing about—" I gestured helplessly between us, "—this?"

"Yes," he repeated and I stared at him, at a loss for words. "What I don't understand is why you care."

"Because you're my boss!"

"So?"

I growled, pushing his chest lightly so I could climb down off of the desk and shrug my coat on. "So people treat men differently from women. People will talk. They'll wonder how long we've been together, if I got my promotion because of you – it diminishes everything I've worked so hard for."

Julien adjusted his tie and buttoned his suit before

he answered. "But you know that's not true, what does it matter?"

I bit my lip. "It matters because I'm not leaving, unlike you. My professional reputation matters – who's to say this doesn't get back to whoever replaces you? What do you think will happen if they think I'm willing to trade sexual favours for a promotion?"

Jules thrust his hand through his hair before sighing and flattening it again. "I think you're overreacting."

My nostrils flared. "What did you just say?"

Julien cleared his throat, apparently realising his error. "I just meant that—"

"No, it's okay. What you meant came through loud and clear."

"Sephy—" he tried but I shook my head, pushing past him and out of the door and then swearing under my breath when I spotted Eileen up ahead chatting with four other women animatedly. Great, the ship was sinking already.

CHAPTER 14

Sephy

"Are you sure this is safe?" Drew said skeptically as we stepped into the sled and pulled the blankets over our lap. I was doubly toasty with a man on either side of me. Seth fussed with the blankets, making sure we were all tucked in, and I hid a smile at his mother-hen tendencies. It was cute. Yesterday, he'd taken me up the slopes in the ski lift and we'd drank hot chocolate in the chalet up there while we'd admired the view. When the wind had rocked the seat on the way down, he'd held my hand and distracted me with endless questions about what I'd been working on and how my parents were, until we'd been back on solid ground before I knew it. We still had a long way to go, but he was trying and that was what mattered right now.

"Yes," I told Drew. "It's only a short circuit anyway, otherwise we'd get too cold."

The huskies were at the front of the large wooden sled, standing patiently and I couldn't help admiring them. I'd always wanted a dog and huskies were just so beautiful.

Seth looked over at me and smiled. "Admiring the pups?"

"Yes." I sighed. "The flat's not big enough for a dog, although I've been thinking about moving out of London."

"You have?"

I looked away, uncomfortable. "London's not as much fun when you're by yourself and I wouldn't mind commuting to work if I found a more affordable place to rent."

"You'll need a bigger place eventually anyway," Drew said and I looked at him in confusion. "Well, you've got three boyfriends now, gorgeous. Where will we all fit?"

Boyfriends. It felt crazy that we were already in that place, but right.

"Well you won't be moving in just yet, that's for sure," I said quickly and Drew smirked.

"I was just talking about sleepovers, but good to know where your head's at."

I felt the heat rising to my cheeks and wanted to swear, so I did, quietly under my breath, and Seth chuckled at my embarrassment.

The guide for the tour settled in front of us to guide the dogs and we started moving with a jolt that made my stomach swoop. Apparently we would be going through the forest on a circuit that would take us past a frozen lake and some mountains, and the snow was pretty light so I was hoping we wouldn't get too cold. I'd stuffed some of those temporary hand warmers into my snow boots to keep my toes warm in the meantime and the blankets were thick and soft.

Drew still looked unsure, holding onto the side tightly as the trees went past us. We weren't really going that fast, but he looked nervous all the same. "How much are we paying for this again?"

"My treat," I insisted and that distracted him from his fear for a moment as his head whipped toward me.

"What?"

I laughed lightly and kissed him on the cheek. "It's okay to let someone take care of you for a change." He didn't say anything but I was pretty sure it was shock that held his tongue as he stared at me. I snorted as I tilted his chin gently to face the scenery going by. "You're going to miss the view."

He turned back to me, a sort of wonder in his eyes. "I'm already looking at the best one there is."

I rolled my eyes but couldn't hold back my smile as Seth shot Drew a look that told him just how cheesy that line had been. I didn't care though, a little bit of cheese wasn't necessarily a bad thing.

"You didn't mention yesterday," I said, turning to look at Seth, "have you stopped in to see your parents since you've been back in London?"

He shook his head. "No, I didn't have time before we flew out here. I'll be seeing them in the new year once the conference is done." Suddenly his cheeks looked pinker as he looked away from me. "You, ah, could come with me if you wanted? You know my mum's always loved you."

He wasn't lying, I'd always got on great with his parents, but it was a big step to take so soon. "Yeah, maybe." I kissed him on the cheek so he'd know I wasn't trying to fob him off and Seth relaxed, giving me a small smile.

The sound of the huskies' paws hitting the soft packed snow was oddly soothing, the rhythmic beating making me snoozy even as the cold air and pretty views kept me enraptured. Half of me thought I could live somewhere like this forever, but the rest of me knew I'd probably be craving sunshine and booty shorts sooner rather than later. But the views might be worth a little sun-craving.

The trees thinned out as we approached a wide open space and I realised I'd misread the brochure – we weren't going past a frozen lake, we were riding on it. I opted not to give this detail to Drew who looked like he was finally starting to relax, looking up at the mountains that towered on either side of the lake with awe.

The snow paused for a little while and we could see a little more of the surprisingly blue sky above us before thick, white flakes began to pour down again. The guide occasionally pointed out things he thought might be of interest, like a mountain valley that experienced hikers apparently liked to take, but mostly he let us enjoy the ride in relative quiet. We paused once we got to the otherside of the lake and the dogs panted happily as we took some photos before climbing back into the sled.

We started to do a loop, going slightly further up past the lake and if I remembered rightly, we would come back through the forest again from the other side until we picked up our original trail. I smiled as I looked between Drew and Seth but it faded when Drew turned to look at me.

"Have you spoken to Jules yet?"

I frowned. I hadn't spoken to or seen him in a couple of days, not since Eileen had found us kissing in the conference room. Of course, that was probably because I'd been avoiding him. But the silence was starting to bother me. I could only assume that he was trying to give me space, even if it meant he was unhappy – because that was just who Julien was. "No," I said shortly and Drew sighed.

"I wish you two would just kiss and make out already."

"I think it's *kiss and make up*," Seth said dryly and I snorted.

"I know. I'll talk to him," I promised and Drew relaxed, an easy smile falling across his face, but there was a little mischief in there too.

"You're so good, Sephy," he whispered in my ear, his warmth breath tickling but also stirring up a not entirely unwelcome sensation lower down too. "I think you deserve a treat."

My eyes widened. Right here? I'd given him a blowjob in semi-public, but we were in the woods!

Nobody would have seen us. But the guide for the tour was *right there.*

"I'm not sure—"

"You can keep quiet, can't you?" Seth murmured and I blinked at him in surprise, not expecting him to get in on this too. He'd never really been against PDA when we were together, but we hadn't pursued it either. Though, I suppose this wasn't quite the same thing as a public kiss. "I can help you," he assured me, bringing his lips to mine and I sighed into his warmth, relaxing and only jumping a little as Drew's cold hand slid under the blankets and unzipped my coat, pressing his chilly fingertips to my skin and grinning when I shivered.

"Have you ever used ice cubes before?" Drew murmured and I turned to look at him like he was an idiot.

"Of course I have."

He laughed and the promise in it made my pussy clench. "No, I mean, down here," he cupped me over my underwear and my hips shifted restlessly as I let out a little gasp.

"Everything okay?" The tour guide called back and Seth smirked.

"Naughty girl, you need to be quiet or we'll get caught," he said quietly before calling louder, "Everything's fine, just a chill."

I shot him a glare and he grinned back but all thoughts emptied from my head as Drew pressed a cold finger to my clit. Seth's mouth covered my own, swallowing my moan as Drew rocked his hand, circling his fingers through the wetness that was quickly gathering for him before dipping one finger inside me.

"That's right, baby. Keep nice and quiet while I fuck you like this, okay?" Drew was watching my lap as if he could see what he was doing to me through the blankets and I bit my lip as he added a second finger. "Seth, why don't you help me out?"

Seth looked at me and I nodded eagerly as his hand slipped under the blanket too, replacing Drew's fingers on my clit so he could focus on working them in and out of me in a rocking motion that quickly had me whimpering.

They took it in turns kissing me, swallowing my cries quickly as my hips tried to press my pussy down harder onto Drew's fingers.

"If I didn't think it would freeze off, I'd give you my dick right here, baby. But you'll just have to wait. Think of it as another treat for after you and Jules make up, hm?"

"O-Okay," I managed to gasp and Drew's smile turned wicked as he added a third finger.

"Are you close, love?" Seth rolled my clit in the way he knew undid me and more than anything I wished I could have his mouth on me again, it was an effective way to keep him quiet. I almost smirked at the thought before a wave of pleasure made me moan his name.

"Yes."

"Good," Drew said, "I'm ready to taste you." He curled his fingers inside of me and I would have screamed if Seth hadn't taken it for himself, silencing the sound with his mouth and tongue until my legs stopped shaking. Drew pulled his hand out of the blanket and smirked at me as he sucked each finger clean. "It's okay gorgeous, you've got some time to recover before round two."

I was panting almost as hard as the huskies and Seth laughed at whatever expression I wore.

"Some husky ride," I breathed and smiled when they did.

"Didn't doubt it would be for a second," Drew quipped and I snorted as we made our way back onto the original trail that led to the resort.

CHAPTER 15
Sephy

I'd promised Drew and Seth yesterday afternoon that I would talk to Jules, and it was a promise I had every intention of fulfilling. So after meeting Noel for breakfast the next day, I set out toward the lodge, knowing Julien would be there alone thanks to Drew's incessant prodding that I talk to him. Seriously. He'd texted me at least ten times since breakfast to ask if I was at the lodge yet – how he was getting away with that during a board meeting, I had no clue.

I'd brought my laptop along so that I could try and keep some of my pride intact and give myself an excuse to talk to Jules. Maybe he was right, maybe I had overreacted, but him telling me that hadn't been super helpful in the moment.

I knocked on the door to the lodge and breathed out slowly, nervousness coiling in my stomach as footsteps padded towards me. It swung open and Julien's shadowed eyes widened in surprise.

"Sephy," he said, relief colouring his voice and I forgot all about my earlier irritation and nervousness as I took in his bedraggled appearance. His shirt was misbuttoned and creased and dark circles surrounded his eyes. I stepped forward and took his face in my hand, looking at him with worry.

"Are you okay? What happened?"

"Just haven't been sleeping well," he said evasively and a stab of guilt hit me, wondering if it was because of our fight. I pressed a kiss to his cheek and let him fold me in his arms for a moment before he stepped back to let me in, closing the door gently behind us.

"I, um, brought my laptop." I held it up in its case for emphasis and something similar to disappointment crossed his face. "But I also wanted to apologise for before. Maybe I did overreact."

He shook his head and I toed off my snow boots before following him into the lounge and taking a seat at the dining table. "No. I'm sorry, you were right. I shouldn't have assumed that it wouldn't be a big deal, or dismissed you like I did."

I smiled and we both relaxed. "We were both idiots," I said and he cracked a smile.

"So you've been working on your presentation?"

I nodded and unzipped my pink laptop case, setting it down on the table and loading up the slides I'd prepared. Jules looked through them with me, pausing to ask a question here and there as he read through the notes, or clarify a point with me. Then we moved on to rehearsing it.

Julien checked the stopwatch on his phone and considered me. "I think the sweet spot for this is probably somewhere between five and ten minutes. Any longer than that and you'll have lost their attention, but any shorter than five and the presentation might not seem detailed enough."

I nodded thoughtfully. "See, this is why I needed you to look at it. I hate public speaking so I avoid it, but that also means I don't have as much experience. Not like you."

Jules shrugged. "I have experience, yeah, but only out of necessity. I don't particularly enjoy giving speeches, it's tedious."

"You looked like you were enjoying the talk you gave to the group the other day though."

"That's different." He rubbed absently at his eyes and my heart melted when he stopped and they looked all sleepy. "That's actually interacting, not just talking at someone."

"Maybe that's what I need to do for this presentation, be more conversational, engage them to hold their attention. Maybe it'll make me feel less nervous too."

Jules stood and stretched, revealing a tantalising glimpse of his stomach. "You don't need to be nervous, you're going to kill it." He ran his hands through his hair, leaving it sticking up wildly and I couldn't take it any more.

"Come on." I held out my hand as I stood and he took it, looking adorably confused as I led him upstairs.

He followed me all the way to his room and looked a little distressed when I started taking off my clothes. "Take your clothes off."

"Sephy… I don't know, I'm a little tired—"

"Trust me?"

He looked at me steadily for a second before reaching down and yanking his top up and over his head without undoing the buttons. I don't know why I found that hot, but I did. He took a step toward me once he was naked and I shook my head, gesturing to the other side of the bed and he obeyed, looking confused as I climbed in on the other side.

"What are we doing?"

"Cuddling." I pressed my back to his front and felt him instantly harden against my arse.

He cleared his throat. "Um, sorry."

"Shhh," I admonished. "Spoon me."

Jules' arms slid around me and once we were tightly wrapped together, he breathed out a deep sigh, his muscles going slack. "Now what?"

"Nap time." He tensed, as if surprised, and I giggled. "You clearly need some rest, Jules. Sleep with me. Just sleep."

He didn't reply and I smiled to myself as I realised from his deep, steady breathing, that he'd already fallen asleep.

I woke up when another body slid into the bed, a sweet, musky cologne washing over me, and I murmured sleepily as Drew pressed a quick kiss to my mouth. He wriggled about until I cracked open an eyelid and found him sprawled out next to me.

"Are you naked?"

"Yes." I grinned. "Want to see?"

"Is Jules naked too?"

"Yes." I considered him. "...Want to see?"

Drew snorted. "No, thanks. I take it you guys kissed and made up?"

"More like kissed and napped."

"And we would still be napping if it wasn't for the strange man who climbed into my bed," Julien grumbled and I grinned.

"You're grumpy in the morning," I teased, squeezing his butt. At some point he had obviously rolled away from me and on to his front, burying his face in his pillow.

"Well, it's technically seven at night but—"

I swatted at Drew before batting my eyes at him hopefully. "Dinner?"

"Seth's on it."

Pleased with that answer, I rewarded him with a kiss that he immediately deepened.

"No, no. I probably have nap breath."

Drew shrugged. "Smell fine to me."

I eyed him suspiciously but let him kiss me again, his tongue against mine waking me up faster than him jumping into bed with us had.

"You two are suspiciously quiet," Julien muttered as he rolled over and watched as Drew slid a hand over my hip and squeezed my arse.

I laughed, breaking our kiss to roll towards Jules. "Nothing suspicious about it, really." Drew attempted to coax me back to him, kissing my neck as Jules captured my attention. His eyes seemed clearer, more well-rested, and I stroked my fingers through his hair gently before kissing him.

"I'm feeling a little left out," Drew complained and I smirked.

"I'm not giving you any more attention until you're naked too."

Drew jumped out of bed so quickly the duvet fell and Jules and I immediately yelled as the cold air rushed over us. "I didn't know that was a requirement, but I'm happy to oblige."

Julien made undressing an art, but Drew made it an exercise of speed. It felt like I'd only blinked and he was suddenly naked and climbing back into bed with us.

"Better?" he asked and I rolled again, letting Jules press against me from one side as I faced Drew on the other.

"Much," I murmured and then his lips found mine again as Jules pressed kisses to my shoulders and neck. Drew's hand grazed the edge of my breast and I gasped when he repeated the motion, small pinpricks of pleasure stirring inside me. I didn't need to check to know that we were all on the same page – Drew was already hard, his erection jutting up toward my stomach, and I could feel Jules' hard length pressing against the small of my back. He shifted lower and started to rock against my arse and my breathing sped up.

"This is both so cosy and so hot," Drew moaned and I laughed breathlessly as his head dipped to lick one of my nipples. His hand stroked down my body and I whimpered when his fingers tested my pussy, feeling for my wetness at the same time that Jules kissed my neck.

Julien rolled away from us and I protested, reaching out a hand but dropped it when he turned back to me, a bottle of lube in his hand. I hadn't been expecting it, but I was intrigued to say the least.

Drew distracted me with a roll of his fingers against my clit and my hips began to rock steadily against his palm, craving more. Jules fulfilled my unspoken need, slicking his index in the lube he'd picked up from his bedside and pressing it against my rear, stroking the tight hole there before working his finger in.

I gasped at the twin pressure, revelling in the feel of them working in tandem on either side of me. I reached my hand between us, catching a hold of Drew's cock and tightening my grip before I stroked him, paying close attention to his head where I knew he was the most sensitive. His breath left him in a rush that made me feel smug as I increased the pace of my hand. But it was my turn to moan when he did the same, adding a second finger to my pussy and bringing me closer to the edge as Jules methodically did the same.

"What do you think, Jules? Is she ready for us?" Drew said tightly, trying to remain in control as I worked him.

"Yeah, I think so." Jules nipped at my neck playfully and I shivered. "Do you want to stay as we are, or switch?"

"Let's stay," Drew said and my breasts tightened in anticipation as I rocked between their fingers eagerly. They withdrew and I bit back my protest as they instead lined themselves up against me, Jules passing Drew the lube over my shoulder and I shivered at the cool feel of it.

"Ready, angel?" Jules's voice was rough with desire and I ached for him as I nodded, waiting for that first push, the initial sting and stretch that I knew would give way to pleasure. Julien groaned as he began to push inside my arse in shallow thrusts, his breathing heavy against me, and I squirmed, ready for more.

Drew's eyes met mine and his smile was slow. "More?"

"Yes," I rasped out, trying to organise my thoughts and failing as Jules increased the pace behind me.

Drew reached between us, stroking my clit as I trembled for them before he started to push inside me. Julien slowed a little so I could get used to the sensation, Drew pushing in as Jules retreated and vice versa until I was trembling between them. Our pants and groans joined together in the air as our bodies rocked. The bed creaked ominously and I laughed a little until the boys switched their tempo, thrusting into me in tandem and I couldn't do anything except pant their names in a high pitched scream.

"I love the way you moan for us, darling." Julien tilted my face to his and kissed me, our tongues twining before he turned my head back to Drew, offering me to him as Jules reached around my body to stroke my breasts, pinching and rolling my nipples. The extra stimulation was too much, if he kept going I was going to explode.

Drew could see I was close, could likely feel me clenching around his cock as he pounded me relentlessly, and reached down to stroke me. I came with a sharp cry. It felt like it went on and on, the boys wringing all of the pleasure out of me until I sank into the bed between them, panting and boneless.

We caught our breath for a second before stumbling to the bathroom to clean up. My legs felt like jelly but I knew the warm water of the walk-in shower would probably help.

I turned on the water and stepped under the spray, pleased when they both stepped into the shower with me too. Jules lathered up my hair as Drew soaped up my chest and I gave him an amused glance. "Are you planning on cleaning me anywhere other than my boobs?"

Drew looked at me in mock outrage. "I'm just being thorough!" His hand dropped as he washed between my legs. "Is that better?" He smirked and I rolled my eyes, gripping his hand by the wrist as I retrieved it from between my thighs.

I reached for the shower gel and soaped him up in turn, enjoying the feel of his dark chest hair under my palms as it became foamy. I moved so he could stand under the spray of water and wrapped my arms around Julien so I wouldn't shiver too much. The steam was warm, but it was still nicer being under the water.

Unfortunately, Drew was a shower hog and I had to distract him with a kiss before I could squeeze my way under again to rinse out my shampoo.

Julien gasped and I turned to him in alarm. "What's wrong?"

"We didn't use a condom! How could I have been so stupid?"

Drew went pale and Jules looked sick. I snorted. "We're fine, I take the pill."

"You do?" Drew propped a hand against the wall like relief had made him dizzy. "Way to get my heart going, Julien."

I pulled them close to me, wrapping an arm around each of their waists as I rested my head on Jules' shoulder. "Sorry, I should have mentioned it before."

"I know how you can make it up to us…" Drew grinned and I flicked water at him in response, but couldn't help the kernel of interest that flared inside me. He saw and smiled wider.

"Ugh, do you think this is the honeymoon period or something?" I whined as I stood back under the water and admired the way the droplets beaded on

Julien's skin. "We can't possibly be this horny all the time. We'll… I don't know, die or something."

"Die from horniness?" Julien smirked and I nodded emphatically.

"Yeah, of like sheer exhaustion, or… Why are you laughing?"

Drew kissed me, it was wet and sloppy but I didn't mind as he continued chuckling. "I just think you're funny."

Julien shut off the water and bravely stepped out into the cold air to retrieve the towels.

"My hero." I beamed up at him as he wrapped me in the towel before slinging one around his waist and whipping the other at Drew.

Jules cuddled me into him and Drew joined us on my other side, resting his cheek against my hair as I shivered. It was quiet except for the trickle of the water draining and the drip of our bodies onto the floor and my heart felt so full that it scared me a little.

"I wonder where Seth is, I'm hungry," I said, mostly to distract myself from the thoughts swirling through my brain. I didn't know where the guys really stood with me. Everything was still too new to be saying anything… drastic.

"I'm sure he's on his way," Julien murmured and Drew nodded.

"But I can think of something to do in the meantime," Drew added and I pulled back to look at him incredulously.

"Again?"

"I miss you." He pouted at me and widened his eyes, drawing my attention to a freckle I'd never noticed before beneath his eyebrow. I tapped it lightly and his lips curved.

"I'm right here."

"Yeah but, I miss the taste of you. On my tongue."

I snorted. I loved Drew's goofy side, he was surprisingly unserious for a guy who, on paper, seemed intimidating.

"Are you saying you don't want to ride my face?" Drew kissed my lips and then my cheek, trailing down to my jaw and my neck. I bit my lip and he grinned, reaching down and cupping my pussy, stroking his thumb down the centre of me. "You're already soaked, gorgeous. Don't you want my tongue inside you?"

I swallowed hard. "I guess it would pass the time while we wait for Seth," I said, attempting to sound nonchalant.

Drew smirked. "Great idea." He bent down, his towel falling to the floor as he lifted me up. I squealed, wrapping my arms around his neck and my legs around his waist as he carried me back to the bed.

"Be careful, I might be—"

Drew kissed me, stopping my words short. "Light as a feather, gorgeous. Is that why Jules calls you angel? Because you're such a good girl?" I blushed and Drew traced the colour over my cheek with a fingertip.

Julien walked into the room, having followed us at a more sedate pace, but he looked on in interest as Drew laid back against the bed and crooked a finger at me.

The mattress bounced a little as I crawled over to him and Julien made a pained sound. I glanced behind me to find his eyes on my arse and I grinned.

"Sephy…" Drew called impatiently and I moved a little quicker, coming up to my knees before him, and he patted the space on either side of his head. "Lean forward and use the headboard if you like."

I nodded, a little worried about suffocating him, but Drew didn't hesitate as I lowered myself. His mouth clung onto my pussy, his tongue immediately moving over me like he'd been dying of hunger and this was what he needed to be satiated.

My hips began to rock, at first gently, but then harder as his hands clutched my thighs and small moans broke free from his mouth. He really was getting off on this, on *me*, I realised with no small amount of wonder.

The bed dipped as Julien joined us, his dick already hardening as he reached for the lube.

"You look so good together," he said, eyes like molten ice as he watched me rock on Drew's tongue. "Can I join you?"

I wasn't sure what he wanted to do, but I nodded anyway because this was Julien and I trusted him completely.

Jules pressed a cold finger to my rear and my eyes widened at his intent as he withdrew and aligned himself. I shifted forward so I could balance better using the headboard and let out a loud moan at the first push Julien made inside my arse as I rode Drew's mouth. God, I half-wished this room had a mirror because I knew we had to look hot as hell right then.

"Well, I came bearing food, but I can see you've made do with a different kind of feast," came an amused, deep voice from the doorway.

I glanced up and smiled when I saw Seth. I opened my mouth to greet him but only a moan escaped as Julien fucked me, our bodies slapping together as Drew opened his mouth wider, sucking on my clit so hard I almost saw stars.

"Do you have room for one more?"

I was half-tempted to say no, to make him look but not touch, to punish him a little longer. But I wanted Seth, and so the only person I'd really be hurting was myself.

I raised a hand and beckoned him forward, my eyes taking him in eagerly as the bed bounced under the weight of the three of us. Seth shrugged off his coat and stepped out of his jeans and boxers. A wet patch had appeared at the front of his boxers and I smirked, knowing we had caused it.

"Where do you want me?"

"Mouth." My voice was hoarse and Seth raised an eyebrow.

"How long have you guys been going?"

Julien chuckled and then moaned as Drew did something with his tongue that made my body clench around him. "This is already round two."

"Well I'm glad I arrived in time."

Seth pumped himself slowly as he watched us, his

eyes hot as he watched me toss my head back and moan, luxuriating in the way they were making me feel.

He stepped up onto the bed and I smiled up at him taking his dick out of his hand and into my own as I finally got to touch him. "I missed you."

"I missed you too," he whispered and despite the heat of what was clearly fucking, there was a tenderness there too. I felt it even more strongly now that we were all together.

I licked the tip of him, taking my time and showering his head in attention as I sucked and moaned and Seth's hands balled into fists.

I was getting close to orgasming, could feel it building quickly, and knew the time for teasing was over if I wanted us all to finish at the same time. I glanced down and Drew winked at me as his tongue plunged into my pussy, making me shout his name. His hand worked himself, wetness gleaming at his tip. He was close too.

I wrapped my mouth around Seth's cock, looking up at him as I did so in the way that I knew he loved. He bit his lip as I worked my way down and back up his shaft, humming as Jules thrust faster and my inner muscles began to tighten.

I flicked my tongue over his head as I tasted Seth and his hips jolted before rhythmically rocking into me. I leaned into it, letting him know what I wanted and he didn't hesitate, sinking his hand into my hair before he began to fuck my face.

I moaned around him as we moved in tandem, each of us growing frantic as we chased the approaching crash down to earth. Jules was the first to break and it was like a chain reaction as he filled me from the back and Seth shouted as he came in my mouth. A warm splash hit me as Drew finished and it was the last that pushed me over.

I trembled in their arms, propped up against every one of the men in my life as the orgasm slowly ebbed away and I tried to catch my breath.

"Welcome home," I mumbled to Seth who smiled before pressing a kiss to my forehead.

"I hope the food's not cold," Drew said, stretching his arms out and then stroking a hand down my back and we all laughed when Julien's stomach grumbled in response.

"Come on," Jules lifted me off of Drew and kissed me softly. "Let's get you cleaned up and fed."

Sweeter words had never been spoken and it made me wonder, as each of them petted my hair or kissed my skin, taking care of me, always taking care of me, just how far my feelings had grown.

CHAPTER 16
Julien

Once upon a time, Christmas Eve had been my favourite day of the year. I'd loved it more than birthdays, more than Christmas Day, and a hundred other holidays. It was the one day a year my father had insisted on keeping to family tradition, in memory of my mother.

So every year, without fail, we watched movies, drank hot chocolate, stuffed ourselves silly with food and listened to music – it was like making up for the entire year of quality time lost in one sitting. Not that he was a bad father, really, he was just busy, but it was hard to grow up with someone and still feel like you don't really know them.

This was the first Christmas Eve in a long time that I'd spent without him. Running the conference, entrusting it to me for the first time, I suspected was a test. I just wasn't sure what for. Did he want to check my dedication? My commitment? Or had he suspected

I was unhappy and was trying to prompt me into making a decision?

Honestly, there was no guessing what went through my father's head sometimes. For all I knew, he just really hadn't fancied running the event this year.

Sephy had been preparing all day to give her big presentation to the board, to show us all the benefits of the new initiative we were letting her put into place and how it could affect the broader business. She'd paced around the lodge endlessly that morning, staring at her notes and murmuring the words to herself. I hadn't been lying when I'd told her she would kill it, she put in the work and it always paid off.

Several of the board members had even smiled when she thanked them for listening.

Sephy glowed, like a beacon of light that had been drawing me in for a long time, but here, now, at the annual Christmas party, she was effervescent.

This was the part of the conference people generally looked forward to, unless they liked to ski, of course. I'd only been up to the slopes once, having been kept pretty busy this time around both with work and Sephy. But the annual party was a good time, open bar, free food, that was usually enough to satisfy people. This year, the London office had voted for a specific addition though.

"Youuuu can daaaance—" Drew crooned into the microphone as he shimmied a little and I could see Sephy laughing with her friend as they watched. He'd found a santa hat somewhere and threw it out into the crowd dramatically, a couple of women even dove for it. I rolled my eyes and Drew blew me a kiss.

Karaoke. I couldn't think of anything worse. Especially as the night progressed. Generally, the more alcohol one consumed, the worse the music tended to get. I wasn't sure how much worse it could get than Drew though, he was truly terrible.

Tomorrow would be a quiet day, some people too hungover from the party to do anything but eat some food and sleep. The others who brought family with them usually spent the day in the lodges opening presents and whatever else families did on Christmas Day. I, on the other hand, had booked a surprise for Sephy and the guys.

A space had been cleared opposite the small tables and temporary stage so that people could dance to the DJ when no karaoke was being done. I desperately wanted to ask Sephy to dance, but I wasn't sure she would say yes. She saved me the trouble a moment later by standing up with Noel and making her way to the dance floor, her curves looking delectable in a red shiny dress with matching heels.

"Are you going to stare at her all night or are you coming to dance?" Seth taunted as he slapped me on the back and strode up to Sephy on the dance floor.

Fuck it. If Seth could dance with her, so could I.

Sephy laughed at something Seth said and then her face lit up when she saw me walking towards her too. Drew's rendition of *Dancing Queen* thankfully ended and I knew he would be following suit to join us.

"You look beautiful," I said into her ear, leaning down so she could hear me over the next song playing.

"So do you!" Her smile was bright and my heart thumped unevenly for a second.

"I have a surprise for you later, and the others too. When you're done here, pack a bag, okay?"

Excitement made her big blue eyes grow large and she beamed. "Okay! But I, um, didn't get you anything."

I laughed. "I forgive you."

Drew ambled over and started moving his hips to the beat before he slung an arm around Sephy's waist. "Did you know they have tequila at the bar?"

Seth and I shared a concerned look. "I don't think that's a good idea, pal."

Sephy raised an eyebrow at me and I winced. "I'll tell you later." The last time Drew had tangled with tequila things had become… messy. I wasn't keen on a repeat and, judging by the look on his face, neither was Seth.

Drew swayed to the music, pulling Sephy along with him until she giggled. The DJ called out, asking for any more karaokers and Seth nudged me. "Aren't you going to have a go?"

I glared at him. "I don't sing." Bastard. It had been *one* time when we were at college and I'd sworn everyone to secrecy afterward.

Sephy had clearly heard him though and perked up. "Oh, go on, Jules. Not even for me?" she said when she saw me grimace.

Her pout transformed into a smile when I reluctantly nodded. Damn. I could not say no to that woman.

I dragged my feet as I walked over to the stage, wanting to delay this for as long as possible, but unfortunately the DJ was over-enthusiastic, or maybe just wanted a break, because he practically salivated when he saw me walking over.

I sighed as the guy leaned down to better hear me over the mix he'd been playing.

"What'll it be?"

My mind went blank and my mouth dry. "Um, you choose."

If his smile had gotten any wider his cheeks would have split. "Excellent, excellent, up you go!"

"Oh, you can finish your song—"

"—Let's give a hand to our newest singer…?" the DJ looked at me and I raised the microphone he thrust out to me reluctantly.

"Julien."

"Julien!" The DJ repeated with a lot more enthusiasm than me. "Take it away!"

I grimaced at Seth in the crowd and he smiled smugly. The music queued and I raised a surprised eyebrow in the DJ's direction. Buble. How original. It was a slow one too, so now I had to serenade the room while Seth got to slow dance with our girl.

"I'll be home for Christmas…" I started and Sephy froze in between Seth and Drew, spinning around to look at me. This was why I didn't sing. It was embarrassing in a way that giving a public speech somehow wasn't. I could feel myself *blushing* for fuck sake.

Instead of dancing, Sephy stared up at me like she was entranced. So I ignored everyone else in the room and focused on her, my voice finding the low notes easily as I completed the run that Buble made sound so effortless.

I wasn't always hugely good at voicing my emotions, and singing was often so raw that I hated performing. But seeing the smile on Sephy's face, the way she swayed absently between Seth and Drew while she watched me, made it worth it. I would sing a thousand songs up on this stage as long as she kept looking at me like that.

"Give it up for Julien!" the DJ called as my song ended and enthusiastic applause rang out. I raised a hand in thanks as I hurried off the stage.

"They didn't clap for me like that," Drew said with mock outrage and Sephy pressed a quick conciliatory kiss to his lips, intriguing me. So she didn't mind a little PDA with Drew, even though he was on the board. Yet she was still so careful around me. Why?

"I do believe it's my turn to dance." I let my hand slide to her hip, feeling the tantalising warmth of her skin through the silky dress and wanting to pull her close.

Sephy didn't protest, just linked her arms around my neck as *Last Christmas* started playing. I could see us getting a few looks, most notably from Eileen – her eyes were narrowed and I made sure to keep Sephy's back to her. I wanted this to be a fun night, I didn't want some idle gossip to ruin that.

"Your voice is gorgeous," Sephy said quietly. "Is there anything you're not good at?"

I smiled briefly. "I'm pretty sure I couldn't stand up in those heels you're wearing."

She laughed breathlessly as I twirled her and it felt like the world disappeared as I pulled her back into my arms and her eyes met mine.

My heart pounded wildly but I didn't try to hold back as I opened my mouth. "Sephy, I need to tell you something."

A small furrow appeared between her brows as she looked at me with concern. "What is it, Jules?"

I blew out a breath, hoping she didn't hear how shaky it was, but I needed to say this, she needed to know that whatever it was that we were doing, it wasn't casual for me. "You don't have to say it back, I just need to say it, okay? I—"

"I love you too." The words were quiet, just for me, and for a second I gaped at her before I nodded jerkily.

"Y-Yeah, I love you." The smile that lit up her face would have brought me to my knees if we weren't already holding each other up. "And the others?"

She swallowed, looking about as nervous then as I had felt a second ago. "Them too." Her eyes met mine as she watched for my reaction to her words. "All or nothing."

I smiled, tucking a strand of her hair behind her ear as the song faded. "Works for me."

"What does?" Drew kissed Sephy on the cheek as he cut in between us.

"You and Seth, technically."

Seth rolled his eyes as he approached, having heard the comment. "Right. When are you going to speak to him?" There was no doubt who the *him* was that Seth referred to.

I looked away and caught Sephy's eye. "When the conference is over."

Seth nodded approvingly and his expression matched the one of pride on Drew and Sephy's faces.

"Are you guys ready to get out of here?"

Drew waggled his eyebrows. "I was born ready."

Sephy snorted and I ignored him. "I have a surprise for you all. Pack a bag and meet us in the lobby, okay?"

I kissed Sephy goodbye, not daring to linger when I knew it might make her uncomfortable, and hurried off to put the final part of my plan into place.

CHAPTER 17
Sephy

I had a small overnight bag packed and I felt strangely nervous as I stood in the lobby of the hotel waiting for Julien and the guys. I'd stayed at the lodge with them several times now, but it had been unplanned so I didn't have any of my stuff, somehow packing a bag made things feel more official.

Then again, I supposed it didn't get any more official than *I love you.* It was an emotion that had been creeping up on me, the words floating around in my head whenever Drew was goofy or Seth teased me and Julien… Well, loving Julien had felt inevitable.

Maybe for some people it would be too soon to say words that felt as big as those three, but I didn't want to hold myself back anymore just because something scared me. I'd decided that when Seth had left me, and I wasn't going to change that now that he was back. All or nothing I'd told Jules, and I'd meant it.

The lobby doors slid open and Seth strolled in, smiling when he saw me waiting.

"You ready?"

I nodded, walking over to him and sneaking in a quick kiss as he took my small overnight bag from me. "Do you know where we're going?"

"Nope."

I frowned at him, Seth hated surprises. "And you're okay with that?"

"It's driving me fucking crazy," he said cheerfully and I snorted, drawing up short as I stared at what awaited us outside.

The night air was freezing and I was glad I'd grabbed my coat and scarf when I'd been packing. The snow was only a fine dusting but it was the reindeer and sleigh that had my eyes wide.

"We're going on a sleigh ride?" I looked excitedly at Jules and took a more cautious step toward Drew. He'd been worried about the husky ride, let alone getting in a sleigh, but he seemed fine with it. "Why did we need an overnight bag?"

"You'll see," Julien said, his smile was big and bright and despite the fact that he hadn't left the company yet, he definitely seemed happier since deciding he would leave. Now all he had to do was talk to his father about it, and I was pretty sure that was what worried Jules the most.

We climbed into the sleigh, Seth's hand on my waist steadying me as I stepped up. Just like the husky ride, there were thick fur blankets inside to keep us warm and once we were all settled, Jules pulled out a flask from inside his coat. I huffed out a laugh that fogged the cold air and he grinned as he offered it to me.

I took a sip and it burned, making me cough. Whiskey. I handed the flask to Drew who shook his head before passing it on to Seth, who promptly sloshed some on himself when the sleigh began moving with a harsh initial jerk.

I rested my head against Drew's shoulder as the trees drifted past us, the snow was so bright that it illuminated our surroundings somewhat as we moved through the forest. It seemed like we were heading to the east side of the resort, closer to the ski slopes, and I wracked my brain, trying to remember what was over there that would require an overnight bag. Obviously we were going to stay somewhere, but I couldn't imagine the ski chalets were worth abandoning the lodge for.

But we didn't turn into the ski slopes, instead we continued on past it, following the bend of the snowy lane as the reindeer handler guided us down a slight slope. That was when I saw what was up ahead.

I gasped and Jules smiled. "You booked us an igloo?"

Drew groaned from above my head. "That sounds cold and definitely not an encouraging environment for taking off clothes."

I peered up ahead, craning forward to try and get a glimpse of them before we pulled up. "They're not literal igloos, Drew. The front is made of glass and the back is like a normal cabin."

Drew tugged my chin gently so I would focus on him as he kissed me. "So you're saying I can eat you out under the stars?"

I bit my lip on a smile. "I mean, yeah I guess."

"No," Seth said and I looked up in surprise. "*We* get to eat you out under the stars."

"And the aurora borealis, hopefully," Jules chimed in.

"It's a good night for it," the reindeer guide called back and I blushed, realising that he had heard everything. "Nice and clear, not too much snow."

Drew grinned as he noticed my red cheeks.

The sleigh started to slow as we approached the first line of glass igloos, the snow blanketing everything so fully it was like the world was untouched, peaceful.

We pulled up outside of an igloo that I presumed was ours and Drew helped me down and out of the sleigh. The reindeer snorted, stamping their bony legs as their breath fogged the air.

"Come on, gorgeous." Drew tugged my hand gently as Jules held the door to the igloo open for us. It was made of a solid wood and everything inside followed the same theme. A small electric fire was set into the wall of a small living room and Seth looked smug as he turned it on and we crowded around the warmth after Jules took our coats. He'd always wanted a fireplace in our flat so he was probably living out his fantasy right now.

Drew's arm was draped around my waist and Jules' was around my shoulders and for a second we just stood there together quietly before Julien turned away to put the kettle on and collect our overnight bags and leave them in the bedroom.

"Wow," he said and I strolled over to see what he'd found.

"Wow," I agreed as I stood next to him by the abnormally large bed and looked out of the glass dome at the snow drifting by peacefully. "Thank you for doing this."

"Anything for you."

I slipped my arms around his neck, linking them behind his head as I looked into his eyes. He watched me back just as intensely before leaning in and covering my mouth with his own. "I love you," he said quietly and I smiled before I kissed him again.

"I love you too."

A hint of pink coloured his cheeks as he pulled away. "I'll go and make us some tea."

"Sounds good." I quirked an eyebrow at Drew who stood watching us from the doorway and he walked in as Jules hurried out.

"So he finally said it then?"

"Finally?"

Drew shrugged. "I could tell he was gone for you as soon as I mentioned your name."

I wasn't sure what to say to that, so I stayed quiet and eventually he pulled me close, pressing a kiss to the side of my head.

"What do the lights look like?" Seth said from behind us and I jumped.

"I'm not sure. I've heard they look better on camera than to the naked eye." I swept my gaze over the sky above us thoughtfully. "There's a weird line over there, like a mist almost. Do you think they just appear or do they, like, develop?"

Seth shrugged as he moved to my other side. "I guess we'll find out."

"Hopefully," I murmured and then sighed happily as Seth turned to me, kissing my cheek and down my jaw to my neck. My head lolled back as Drew mimicked him on my other side. I was lost in the warmth of them, the feel of their mouths on my skin, so when Julien joined us and chuckled quietly, I jumped a little.

He stood there in the doorway, watching the three of us with a cup of tea in each hand, one of which he then passed to me. I took it gratefully, I'd been dying for a good cup of tea all this week but the stuff they had in the hotel didn't taste right, slightly too strong, crisp, somehow.

"This is amazing Jules," I said as I blew gently on my steaming drink before setting it down on the side. "I wish I had known to get you guys something before I came on this trip. Maybe I can make it up to you all when we get back home?" I bit my lip, anxious for their answer. "You're staying in the UK for the time being right, Drew?"

Drew's dark eyes locked on mine before he smirked slightly. "I can be persuaded to stay."

"I can be very persuasive," I agreed, stepping slightly away from Seth as I moved closer to Drew. "Will you? Come back with us?"

"I will on one condition."

I held my breath, wondering what he could want – whatever it was, I'd do it to keep him with me. I couldn't tell the future, I had no idea if what was between the four of us would last, but I couldn't walk away without trying. "What is it?"

Drew leaned in, the warm glow from the fire in the other room making his brown skin even warmer as it lit upon his cheek. "A kiss."

I laughed as I released the air I'd sucked in. "That can definitely be arranged."

He grinned and wrapped his arms around me, tipping me back into a fancy dip as he claimed my lips. "I guess that settles it, I'm yours."

I felt like my cheeks ached from smiling so much as he righted me and found Julien watching us with a light in his eyes that made me feel equally gooey.

"And what about you?" Jules asked and I tensed slightly in Drew's arms, kind of glad someone else had asked Seth instead of me. I loved them, all three of them. I'd fallen hard and fast and I wasn't sure I'd ever really let Seth out of my heart in the first place. If he chose to leave again… I would be fine, eventually, but that would be it. I couldn't keep wanting him to choose me and then watching as he left.

A warm hand closed over my shoulder as Seth steered me around so my back was to Drew's front. His eyes were wide and earnest on mine as he took a steadying breath. "I was wrong."

I choked. I could probably count on one hand the amount of times Seth had ever admitted that to me, or anyone. He had a lot of pride and most of the time I found it endearing, other times not so much.

"I never should have left you, I was miserable the whole time I was away."

"The whole time?" I said, doubtfully, and Drew chuckled in my ear, making me shiver.

"The whole time," Drew confirmed. "Was downright depressing to watch."

Seth shrugged half-heartedly. "I love you. I don't think I ever stopped, or that I ever could."

"I think this is the part where you kiss him," Drew murmured quietly enough that only I could hear and I pinched his thigh in response.

Seth got down on one knee and my heart felt like it was in my throat for a second until he also dropped to his second and looked up at me. Noel had told me to make him grovel and Seth had definitely done so.

I offered him my hand. "You don't need to be kneeling down there."

He smirked, his cockiness flooding back as he saw the acceptance on my face. "I'm happy to get on my knees for you whenever you want, Sephy. I don't mind staying down here right now, in fact," he said, voice turning husky. I'd never really given much thought to whether a man crawling towards me would be hot, I could now say definitively that it was.

"I'm sorry," I said roughly and felt three pairs of eyes snap on to me instantly, the pressure of their gaze turning me on. "I think my tea is going to get a bit cold, Jules."

"I'll make you another," he replied, a deeply satisfied look on his face as Seth pushed up the hem of my slip dress, revealing my hips and my bare pussy.

Drew pressed a long, hot kiss to my neck as he reached across me to cup one of my breasts. "I can't believe you weren't wearing underwear this whole time. I could have got you off at least twice on the sleigh ride."

I laughed but it turned into a moan as Seth slicked two fingers through me, curling them inside my pussy when he felt how wet I already was for him. He looked up at me in amusement, eyes twinkling. "We've barely even started and you're already dripping for me, love."

"I guess I like you being on your knees." Julien chuckled and I raised an eyebrow at him. "There's room on the floor for you too, you know."

"You tell him, gorgeous," Drew murmured and I leaned my head back so I could kiss him, shuddering against his body as Seth's tongue joined his fingers.

"I'm afraid it doesn't work like that, angel." Julien finally approached me and I broke away from Drew long enough to watch him, loving the demanding, self-confident smirk he wore. Jules nudged Drew aside and he let me go easily, coming around to stand in front of me instead.

Seth's tongue pressed against my clit, stroking me slowly and I gasped, widening my stance as he buried his face between my legs. Julien looked over my shoulder to watch and nodded approvingly. Then he placed his palm on the centre of my back, urging me to step forward so my thighs were bracketing Seth's head, and then pressed down so I bent over for him.

I let him manoeuvre me, loving the thrill of it and feeling secure in the fact that this was Julien and I trusted him. His palm came down against my left butt cheek, the sharp sting making my pussy unexpectedly pulse and Seth rumbled his appreciation as he reached up to unbutton his shirt around his neck.

"So pretty," Julien said as he stroked my arse and the words sounded like a prayer. "Spread those pretty thighs wider for me, angel."

I obeyed as best I could and Julien pulled his hands away from me as Drew tossed him what I assumed was a bottle of lube. I knew I was right when a cold finger stroked along the tight entrance to my arse before pressing inside.

"You never did show me how you use that toy, Sephy." Jules' voice was a gentle chide and I shivered as Seth flicked my clit with the tip of his tongue before rocking his fingers inside me.

"There's still time," I managed breathlessly and Jules chuckled.

"I'm an impatient man." His finger pulled back

only to be replaced by two that he pushed inside me with no preamble and I gasped at the tug. "Why don't you give Drew some attention while I get you ready for me, darling."

It was a command, one I had no problems about obeying. Drew had been steadily undressing as Seth and Jules kept me preoccupied, his belt was open and his slacks half unzipped, his white shirt lay open and I traced my eyes over his body as he moved closer.

I attempted to raise a hand from Seth's shoulder and promptly wobbled. "I guess my mouth will have to do."

"Oh no," Drew said sarcastically and I laughed. His boxers were a deep grey and I watched eagerly as he reached inside them to palm himself.

"Drew," I whined and he smirked.

"Don't worry, baby. I won't make you beg for it." He tugged his cock free from his boxers and I licked my lips as I eyed the long length of him. "Open wide, sweetheart."

I let my lips part and tried to suck his head before he could thrust in and he moaned when my tongue flicked across his slit. Drew thrust a little deeper and I breathed shallowly to stop myself from gagging as he approached the back of my throat.

"Fuck baby, your mouth feels so good on me." Drew's hand slid into my hair and I didn't complain as his hips moved a little faster.

"You're doing so good, angel," Jules said from behind me, his voice sounded strained from holding himself back and I wiggled my ass slightly in the air to encourage him onward. "You think you're ready, huh?"

Seth pressed his mouth back to my pussy and I moaned around Drew's cock repeatedly as Julien thrust into my arse from behind.

"You're not in control here, darling. I'll fuck you when I say you're ready." Julien thrust in again and my pussy clenched around Seth's fingers. I wanted to point out that despite what Jules said, I'd asked and he'd obeyed, but my mouth was too full of Drew to do anything but groan as they pleasured me from both sides.

One of Drew's hands slid out of my hair and cradled my breast, his fingers rolling one nipple, pinching it until my hips shifted restlessly between Jules and Seth. "Is that good, sweetheart? You look like you're enjoying yourself." Despite Drew's calm words, his breathing was just as laboured as mine as his hips sped up.

"When Drew comes for you, you're going to swallow," Jules said and I bobbed my head faster to show my agreement. "But you're not going to come until we say so."

A flicker of frustration lit in me as Jules kept up his torturously slow pace and Seth pulled back, likely needing to give his mouth a break as he focused more on using his fingers. He smiled at me though so I took that to mean he was good.

"Sephy," Drew said roughly, his hand tightening in my hair as the motion of his hips grew more frantic.

"Now, Sephy," Jules said and finally increased his pace as Drew shouted, spilling into my mouth as he came. I swallowed like Julien said to and Drew looked pleased as his eyes opened dazedly and a sweet smile came across his face.

He leaned down and pressed a sloppy kiss to my mouth before backing away and shedding the remainder of his clothes.

"You did so good." Seth smiled as he rubbed my clit with the heel of his palm while three of his fingers held me at the edge.

"Yes," Jules said breathlessly and I whimpered as he withdrew from my body. "But you don't get to come just yet, angel. I want to ring in Christmas Day with our names on your lips."

CHAPTER 18
Julien

Sephy groaned in frustration as we kept her on the edge without letting her come, her face was beautifully pink and a light sheen of sweat made her shine as Seth stood up and massaged his knees while Drew and I helped her out of her dress.

"You looked so beautiful tonight," I murmured, pressing kisses to her neck and shoulders as we slid her straps down her arms, letting her breasts fall free from the material.

"She looks beautiful every night," Drew protested and Sephy giggled, laughing harder as we struggled to pull the material past her hips.

"Normally I'd pull it up over my head," she said helpfully. "Slightly easier to get past my belly and boobs than my thighs."

We reversed our course and soon she stood naked before us, her blonde hair a little messy and her lips a red colour that looked so fuckable I had to look away before I lost control. Fucking Sephy's mouth wasn't the plan, not right now anyway. I reached for the top button of my shirt, relieved to finally be getting out of it, when Sephy's hand covered my own and she began to work the buttons free herself. I watched her while she did so, admiring the way the low light made her look cosy, warm… like *home*, I realised.

I tipped her chin up and she smiled before I kissed her.

"Not to be that guy," Drew said cheerfully as he pulled several loose hair pins from Sephy's hair and ruffled it up. "But I think I could use a little of that right about now."

I raised an eyebrow and didn't move away, instead turning Sephy so Drew could kiss her as her arse ground backwards into my still-hard dick.

"You're such a tease," I said, smacking her ass and she pulled away from Drew to smirk at me.

"Well, actually you're the one who pulled back before, so I think that makes you the tease." She wasn't wrong.

"It's for your benefit, darling."

Seth stood before her, his hard-on jutting out in a way that had to be painful at this point and I couldn't blame him, if our roles had been reversed I would have been dying for her right now. Hell, I *was* still dying for her.

"We're going to bring you to the edge over and over before we let you come." Seth smiled at her like he hadn't just told her we were going to tease the hell out of her. Sephy pouted but her eyes were alight with challenge.

"You can try," she taunted and I smirked.

"Good idea." I took off the rest of my clothes and reached for her, carrying her over to the bed and laying her on my lap. She squealed and then moaned as she felt me press against her. "Pass me the lube, Drew."

"I'll do it."

"Open your legs for him, angel."

Sephy obeyed and I kissed her, her head tucked beneath my chin as Drew lubed up one of his fingers and began working it in and out of Sephy's arse. Her thigh muscles tightened and I nipped at her mouth in reprimand.

"Don't come yet, darling." She let out a frustrated groan and I chuckled. "I promise you'll thank us for it afterwards."

Having had his fun, Drew passed me the lube and I sat Sephy upright as I worked more of it onto my dick. My hands were a little slippery as I cupped the backs of her thighs and lifted her up and back again, nudging at her back entrance and sinking my head inside of her shallowly at first.

"Who do you want inside your pussy and mouth, angel?"

Sephy's breaths were coming out in pants and I slowed the motion of my hips some more as she tried to answer.

"Seth in my mouth."

I nodded approvingly and thrust upwards hard. It

was a good call, Seth was probably going to explode pretty fast judging by the look of him, but Drew had already come and could make this last a little while longer.

"Oh, oh, oh," Sephy panted as she bounced on top of me and her words became muffled as Seth approached the left hand side of the bed and she took his dick into her mouth. Watching her mouth move was hypnotising and Seth seemed to agree, his eyes barely leaving her face as he watched her suck him.

Drew knelt on the bed, fully naked as he watched my dick moving in and out of her, his gaze hungry, and I nodded in understanding, shifting my legs wider and Sephy a little higher on my chest. Her eyes widened as she watched Drew approach, stroking his dick in his hand as it quickly re-hardened.

"Are you wet for us, baby?" Drew crooned as he stroked between her legs and Sephy moaned her reply as Seth began to fuck her mouth. I had a great view, probably the best one giving that Seth's eyes had fallen shut. Drew slicked his head against her entrance and pushed into her slowly. Sephy's thighs pushed apart wider as she began to eagerly rock against us, her movements frantic, and I stopped moving at the same time as Drew, not wanting her to find release too fast.

Once her breathing slowed a little, we began moving again, fucking her between us. Sephy reached down her body, her fingers aiming for her clit, and I caught her hand, pinning it to her side as Drew groaned.

"If you don't play by the rules," he panted, "we'll punish you." He plunged into Sephy's pussy deeply and circled his hips until she writhed on top of me and just as her muscles tensed, he stopped.

I was impressed Seth had lasted so long, though his control was clearly fracturing. His face was tilted upwards as his hips jerked and his eyes widened when they opened. He pulled away from her for a second and I realised why a second later.

"Sephy, look!"

We all looked up and I could feel Sephy's smile as we watched the aurora borealis light up the sky, dancing through it in greens and purples that made the stars glimmer brightly.

"That's the most romantic fucking thing," Drew moaned, his hips not having slowed for a second as we drove Sephy out of her mind. "God, I love you."

For a second, he looked startled, like he couldn't believe that he'd said those three words at all, let alone that he'd chosen right that moment to do it. But Sephy didn't even hesitate, just turned her gaze from the snowy, bright skies to Drew and beamed at him.

"I love you too."

I shifted my angle slightly and Sephy gave a sharp cry, her hips rocking faster than before as she took Seth back into her mouth.

"Please," she whimpered as she took Seth's dick out of her mouth, small beads of moisture had formed on her skin and her eyelashes were damp as she finally begged us. "Please."

Drew and I thrust in tandem and I could feel the moan she couldn't make around Seth vibrate through her body as we fucked her relentlessly, the lights outside casting a colourful sheen over our bodies as Seth called Sephy's name, filling her mouth.

I felt her arse tighten around me and knew from Drew's hoarse moan that he'd felt the same and then her back bowed as she shook silently, her orgasm erupting with enough force that she took me and Drew along for the ride. For a moment, we all laid there panting, slumped over and Sephy winced as she rolled off of my body and stood up, swaying slightly.

"You okay?" Seth called as she wandered off.

"Yeah, peeing."

He smiled and we watched the lights as we got our breath back.

"This is bed is fucking huge. How did you manage this?" Drew asked after a moment and opened his arms when Sephy walked back in the room. She climbed into them and rested her head on his chest as her hands reached for me and Seth.

"Oh, I requested their orgy cabin," I said sarcastically and Seth snorted.

"This is amazing," Sephy said quietly and a sense of peace settled over the four of us as we watched the sky. I checked my watch and smiled when I saw it was midnight.

"Yeah, it is. Merry Christmas, guys."

They chorused their replies to me and it felt good.

We were still figuring out how to do this with her, how to be together like this, but it felt right.

Sephy lifted her head from Drew's chest and climbed from the end of the bed to the top, still naked, and I told my dick to calm down as I watched her crawl. She tucked herself under the covers in the middle of the bed and we each moved to settle around her.

"Best Christmas ever," Sephy murmured sleepily to me and I melted. I couldn't have agreed more.

CHAPTER 19
Sephy

We'd spent the majority of Christmas Day and Boxing Day in bed, looking up at the sky above us. It was an amazing view and I missed it as soon as we left and headed back to the hotel. We'd had Christmas dinner over at the ski resort restaurant and it had been… okay. But the company had more than made up for it.

Some people were leaving today now that most of the group activities and meetings were over, but those higher up in the company had a few extra days they were needed on-site. I didn't mind really, it was just more time that I could spend with the guys before we flew back to the UK.

I'd called my parents on Christmas Day and had felt nothing but relief that I had missed the party this year. My brother's youngest had been screaming in the background the entire call and we'd eventually given up trying to talk over the noise. I'd promised to visit them once I got home and that was fine, but I wasn't sure what their reactions were going to be when I told them I was no longer single. I'd left for the holidays with no boyfriend and was coming back from Lapland with three.

I'd agreed to meet Noel at the bar before the final meeting of the conference began, after which most people were headed home. I knew Jules was going to be doing a speech and that I'd likely get a kick out of watching him commanding the room again, so it was better that I saw Noel before the meeting otherwise I might be… occupied afterwards.

I'd been waiting for Noel for ten minutes, which was fine, I had been a little early after all, but I'd been getting some strange looks since I'd arrived. It got to the point that I discreetly peered into my glass to see if there was something on my face in the reflection. There wasn't. My skirt wasn't tucked into my underwear and, as best I could tell, I didn't have anything stuck to my back. So I wasn't sure why… A terrible thought hit me. This couldn't be about what Eileen had seen, could it? Come to think of it, I supposed we hadn't been that inconspicuous at the Christmas Eve party. But why should we be?

I had been right to be concerned about people seeing me with Julien and jumping to conclusions, but he'd also been right that he was leaving the company and we hadn't really done anything wrong. And if it was about dating all three of them… Anger started to burn in my stomach and the next woman to give me a strange look I glared at. She baulked and didn't look back again. My phone dinged with a new message and I sighed as I read Noel's message: *Sorry, stuck in a last-minute meeting. Catch up tonight instead?*

I texted her back a quick reply agreeing to a drink later on and stood up from my stall. I could kill some time at the reindeer enclosure before the team meeting began or—

I stumbled slightly as I walked past a table of women a little older than me and caught a few words of their conversation—*so unprofessional, bet she only got this far because she looks good in a skirt.* I hesitated, unsure whether or not to confront them. I mean, really it was a compliment that she thought I was hot enough to seduce Julien. I took a deep breath and strode past without looking at them.

I'd spent too much time as a teen worrying about how other people saw me, what they might be saying, and it had taken a lot of work on myself (and a fair few hours with a therapist) to get to the point that I could be as confident in myself and my body as I was. So why did some small-minded idiots bother me so much?

I realised my hands were shaking with anger and I balled them up as I plopped into a chair in one of the small seating areas that looked out at the snow. Suddenly I had no desire to go out there or see anyone, which was ridiculous, but I guessed some wounds will forever be sore and I just had to keep working to heal them every day.

I didn't mean to sit there for so long, seething and mulling things over, but suddenly Julien was standing in front of me, his eyes crinkled at the corners with concern.

"Hey, I've been messaging you. Everything okay?"

I forced a smile onto my face. He didn't need to know about what those women had been saying, no sense in ruining his day too. "Yeah, just zoned out I guess."

A small smile flitted over his face as he offered me a hand. "The meeting's starting soon. You ready?"

I nodded and accepted his hand, but my smile dropped as I turned to find the same group from the bar sniffing at me like I'd somehow personally offended them.

"Come on," I muttered to Julien when he looked at the group with a furrowed brow. He was smart and I didn't want to linger where he could put together what was going on.

We walked into the same room that the Christmas party had been held in and I spotted Noel standing off to one side and made a beeline for her. She smiled when she saw me and I felt like a load came off my shoulders. Obviously I'd already told her what had happened with me and the other guys, but knowing she didn't care what other people thought about that, or whatever they were spreading, was a relief regardless.

"Sorry I couldn't make it earlier," she said, linking her arm through mine as if she could tell I needed the extra support. "Cocktails later though? My flight doesn't leave until the morning."

"Sounds good." I tried for a smile but dropped it when it wobbled.

Julien stood at the front of the room talking to Drew and when he turned around and looked expectantly out at everyone, people instinctively began to quieten down. Drew winked when he noticed me standing off to the side and my lips quirked up slightly. That was one of the things I liked about Drew, no matter my mood he always made me smile, even if it was just a small one.

"Thank you all for being here this past week and a half. It's been amazing watching you all bond and grow and I'd love to give a big shout-out to Noel for heading up so many of our activities!" Everyone applauded politely and I stiffened as people turned and saw me standing with her. Great. "I hope you all loved the Christmas party too…" Julien went on to thank all the various organisers and supporters of the conference and I tuned him out as I felt eyes on me again. I clapped robotically and then startled when the next name called was my own. "Finally, for those of you who don't already know her, I'd love to introduce Sephy from HR." Jules pointed to me and I waved, a hollow feeling growing in my stomach. "Sephy has been such a tremendous asset to the company this year," Julien began and I heard someone close-by snicker.

"I'll bet," they said, loudly enough that Julien paused before continuing.

"In an effort to bring in the best talent to *Quinnings,*

Sephy has started a new initiative specifically targeting entry-level candidates that benefits both potential employees as well as the company. Not to mention, the new employee incentive program she's introduced too."

"Oh yeah, we all know what kind of incentive she provides." A few laughs rang out and this time Julien definitely heard. His face darkened and I found myself holding my breath.

"Sorry, would you care to repeat that?" he called to the crowd and it was silent until someone coughed around the word *whore*.

I blinked. Idle gossip I'd expected, but this? I never could have imagined this. To be fair, several of the faces around me looked just as shocked. There was no ignoring this, no buying my head in the sand or waiting for people to forget. I needed to nip this in the bud right here and now.

I blew out a deep breath and stepped forward just as Julien opened his mouth. His eyes were a little wide, like he couldn't believe what he'd just witnessed, and I knew exactly how he felt.

I strode towards the front of the room and stood next to Jules, looking out at a sea of faces that turned my stomach for a second. No. Enough was enough.

"I can't believe this needs to be clarified," I began, the same anger from earlier now sizzling in my veins and loosening my tongue as I glared. "But clearly from the whispers and comments I've heard today, it needs to be said." I found Eileen's face in the crowd and set my sights on her until she swallowed hard. "I did not sleep my way into this job. I worked hard for my promotion. I've busted my arse all year to get this new program up and running, sacrificed a lot in the process – I actually almost missed my own birthday party because I was working, as well as the birth of my niece. So for anyone to imply that I slept my way to the top is frankly beyond insulting."

Noel nodded encouragingly but a few of Eileen's pals looked set to pitch a fit.

"We saw you kissing Julien!" One of them called out and I changed my focus to them. Half these people I didn't even know and yet they seemed to hate me so much for what? Kissing a fellow consenting adult?

"Not that I have to justify myself to you," I began and saw Jules shoot me a concerned glance and Noel bite her lip on a grin, "but the relationship between Julien and me is a recent development and—"

"But I saw you kissing the other one!" Another, younger, woman hollered, face turning red in indignation. Were they all just in love with Jules and worried for him?

"I'm dating them all!" I yelled out in frustration, finally just done with this conversation and feeling a numb shock that I was having to have it in the first place with a room full of people I barely knew. "And frankly it's none of your damn busin—"

"I'm leaving the company," Julien announced, cutting me off, and I gaped at him but bit back my words. This was getting out of hand and he'd been right to interrupt but I hated that he had to reveal something so personal just because of some nasty comments and childish behaviour. He hadn't even spoken to his dad yet! But he nodded at me, clearly certain about his decision, so I nodded back as gasps rang out. "I don't yet have a firm leaving date for you all and I would have preferred not to have told you all quite yet, but considering the professionalism of my—very new—girlfriend is being called into question, I'd rather settle this right here and now." Shocked silence settled on the room but I didn't care, I was too busy dissolving into a puddle of goo at Jules' words. *Girlfriend.* It was the first time any of them had said that aloud to other people, I was sure.

Drew and Seth stepped up to my side and I ran an eye across the room again, shaking my head in disappointment, and, to their credit, several of the people who'd poked their nose where it didn't belong looked embarrassed. Idiots.

"Well," Julien said when the silence persisted. "I think we'll just leave it there. Thanks again for coming."

People began to awkwardly file out of the room and Noel walked up to me, an excited gleam in her eye. "That was awful," she exclaimed, "but you did so good."

I sighed. "Thank you."

"She's right," Seth said and I looked up in surprise. "You've changed so much since we were together and I knew that, but the Sephy of a year ago would never have stood in front of a room full of people and told them to piss off."

"I didn't tell them to—"

"Your expression did." Drew grinned and I relaxed as he pulled me close.

"I'm proud of you," Seth said, his voice soft and I took a deep breath as I looked into his eyes.

"You're right," I said slowly. I nodded decisively. I didn't feel like I'd done the wrong thing, in fact, I felt… proud, for sticking up for myself and for the people I loved. "I'm proud of *you*," I said, as I walked closer to Julien. "I know that's not how you wanted to tell people, but you actually put yourself first for once." I kissed him before he could respond and his hands fell to my waist as he held me to his chest.

"Thank you," he whispered against my lips and I kissed him again.

"Anytime."

The boys closed in around me and Noel smiled as she backed away with a quick wave. I nodded to her and just let the three of them surround me as we leaned on each other.

"I love you," I said and smiled when a chorus of *Iloveyous* rang back at me.

Epilogue

SEPHY

"Darling! You're—" my mother checked her watch and gaped at me, "—early!"

I snorted. It was true that I didn't think I'd *ever* been early to the family Christmas party before, but Julien liked to be punctual no matter the occasion and I was inclined to indulge him – especially considering he'd given me head for an hour this morning. He'd also been incredibly helpful in the shower while Seth attempted to make us all breakfast. I hadn't exactly downsized my flat like I'd planned, but with three boyfriends… I needed the extra space.

"Merry Christmas." Drew smiled easily at my mum and I watched her melt, he just had that way about him. It had taken my parents a little while to warm up to Seth again after he'd left me before, but soon enough they were getting along fine, though he'd told me that both my mum and brother had separately taken him to one side and threatened him. But aside from that, I'd been surprised at how easy-going they'd been about the four of us.

"Are the kids here yet?" Seth asked eagerly. None of us were particularly set on having a baby ourselves, but I knew that he loved playing the fun Uncle whenever we saw my niece and nephew.

"No," my mum said, stepping back from the doorway to let us in and pressing a kiss to each of our cheeks as we passed by.

"Thank god," I muttered and she elbowed me. "What? I'm just savouring the sanctity of my eardrums being intact for the time being."

Julien chuckled and Drew set down our bag of presents by the tree as Seth helped him unload them.

"How's everything?" she asked me quietly as the guys distracted themselves and I smiled. Truthfully, everything was great. I'd left *Quinnings* six months ago, the atmosphere just hadn't been the same for me after the 'conference showdown' as Drew called it. But I was at a new company, earning more, and the four of us had just found a new place on the outskirts of London.

"Good," I said and when she kept staring at me I laughed. "Very good."

"Is that it? Is that all the details a mother gets from her only daughter nowadays?"

I wrapped my mum in my arms, pressing a kiss to the top of her head. "Don't be dramatic."

"How's the new place?"

"It's gorgeous, you and Dad will have to come and stay soon."

She beamed, appeased by that as I'd known she would be. "That sounds lovely, dear."

My dad walked in and did his manly handshake-back-slap routine with the guys before spotting me and wrapping me into a bear hug. "Hey! Didn't hear you come in."

"Good practice for when the kids get here and we can't hear anything," I teased and he snorted as my mum swatted at my arm.

She drew him away, muttering about potatoes that needed peeling, and I plopped myself down onto the old leather sofa they'd had for years. There was a familiar sort of comfort in being at my parents' place, different to how I felt with the guys at ours. Like there was a nostalgia here that weighed heavily on me.

"You okay?" Julien pressed a kiss to my forehead and I leaned against him as he sat down next to me.

"Perfect." I smiled and looked up to find Drew perching himself on the arm of the sofa.

"Got that right." He blew me a kiss and I pushed him off the sofa.

"My mum will kill you if she sees you sitting on the arm."

"Nah, I think I can take her."

"Charm the pants right off her," Seth mused, wandering over with a drink in hand.

"Ew," I complained and then gestured at his drink, "and how do you have a drink before me?"

"I guess they like me better."

I rolled my eyes but couldn't hold back my laugh as

I looked up at all three of them, marvelling again at how lucky we were to have found each other.

The doorbell rang out repeatedly signalling my brother's arrival and we all froze as we looked in the direction of the hall.

"Let the fun begin," I teased and squeezed Drew's hand. Though truthfully, I suspected this year would be different. Just like me.

Acknowledgments

Thank you so much for reading *Three Kisses More*! I hope you enjoyed spending time with Sephy and her guys. If you get a second to leave a review, I'd be forever grateful! If you want to keep up with my book releases, you can find me on social media or you can sign up to my newsletter so you never miss an announcement. Read on for a free excerpt from *This Never Happened.*

Thank you to Hannah Kaye, my fabulous alpha reader, and Helena V Paris for cheering me on and reading an early draft of this book. You're the best! I'm also sending lots of love to my ARC team who were told about this book a little earlier than the public and had to keep everything hush-hush for the surprise drop —your support is everything and I'm wishing you all the best for the holidays and 2023.

As always, a final thank you to my partner, Connor. You are everything.

About the Author

Jade Church is an avid reader and writer of spicy romance. She loves sweet and swoony love interests who aren't scared to smack your ass and bold female leads. Jade currently lives in the U.K. and spends the majority of her time reading and writing books, as well as binge re-watching The Vampire Diaries.

Falling into bed with your brother's best friend was probably never going to end well...

Chapter One

SARA

This couldn't be happening. My brother's voice continued to rumble through the phone I had pressed tightly to my ear, oblivious to the maelstrom of panic now crashing through me. When I'd reluctantly agreed to go on this trip – mostly to stop Rob's whining – I'd known it was possible *he* was coming, as this was supposed to be a thank-you trip for organizing the wedding. But I'd thought, *It's a big lodge, I'm sure I can avoid him for a week. Maybe he won't even come.* Ha. Apparently Rob (and whoever I'd pissed off upstairs) had other ideas. What could I say though? Um, sorry Rob, but *hell no*?

It would seem like a pretty strong reaction to someone that (as far as he knew) I'd had only a passing acquaintance with and there were a thousand reasons I didn't want to go down that rabbit hole. Firstly, it was none of Rob's business what I did or who I did it with.

Secondly, he was my brother and the thought of talking to him about sex made me want to barf. Lastly… it was hard to simply tell your brother you had a one-night-stand with his best friend. At his wedding. And it hadn't even been worth it.

"Sara? Hel-*lo*, God I swear you are the most – Have you even been listening to anything I've said?" Rob sounded annoyed, it was a tone I was fairly familiar with as it was almost always directed at me and I'd heard my fair share of it back in September when I'd flown out to California to stay with Rob and Tanya for the wedding. Admittedly, on this occasion he was right to be mad, I had tuned out all of his words after *Fletcher will probably be on his way to pick you up by now*. That sort of seemed like information he might have wanted to mention before this whole trip was organised. The fact that I was going to have to spend several hours in the tight confines of Fletcher Harris' car and pretend like we hadn't screwed each other's brains out less than a month ago? Not that Rob knew that last part so he'd probably just thought it made 'economical sense' seeing as Fletcher apparently lived close-by.

"I'm here, I'm listening," I said with a huff of breath, flipping my auburn bangs out of my eyes a little harder than was strictly necessary.

"So, you've packed a swimsuit then, yeah?"

"Erm–"

Rob swore colourfully. "There's a sauna in the

lodge. Bring a suit so I don't have to see your naked ass."

"Sure," was what I said, but internally I was screaming. Pack a *suit*? What swimwear did I even own any more? I lived in *Anchorage,* not Florida. This day was only going to get worse. I'd never even thought to ask Fletcher where he was from, I had just assumed he lived near Robert in Cali. I'd never felt more terrible about being wrong. "Listen, I've got to go, I'll see you at the lodge, right?"

Rob murmured an affirmative and then said sternly before hanging up, "Be nice to Fletch. He's not been himself recently."

Not been himself? Was this me reading into things, or was Fletcher just as unhappy about my presence on this trip as I was about his? Which, honestly, seemed a little unfair – I hadn't done anything besides give him the 'best head of his life' and let's be real, there was no way it wasn't the best sex he'd ever had either. I was there. It was great. The evening up until then had been nice too, we'd laughed together and danced together and I still couldn't shake off the way his eyes had heated when I'd told him I was going to bed.

"Oh," he sounded disappointed as he glanced away from me. "You're tired?"

"Not at all," I'd said with a slow smile and an answering grin had tugged at his mouth as his eyes turned molten. He wanted me and I was more than happy to oblige.

I groaned as I tried to brush the memory away, why did he have to live so close? How had I not known? Well, actually, his surfer-boy tan and blue eyes screamed California, and I had just never questioned it.

Was I even swimsuit appropriate at the moment? I frantically thought back, trying to remember my situation down there when I'd put on panties this morning – I couldn't remember anything too wild and it looked like headlights were approaching outside, so I just had to trust that I'd kept up some form of maintenance downstairs. It was a little risky because I hadn't slept with anyone since Zach, who had been a rebound fling that had fizzled almost as soon as my ass had hit his bedsheets, and I didn't always bother to shave if it was only me, myself, and I heading to orgasm-town, population… one.

I dropped my duffel to the floor and ran to my bedroom to search for some sort of swimwear before the devil himself knocked on the door. It was times like these that I was glad for the lack of stairs in my house, everything on one floor and easily accessible. It made rolling to bed after an ice cream fuelled crime documentary binge so much easier.

I rummaged around in the top drawer of my vanity, pushing aside tights that I hadn't worn in forever and a vibrator that had run out of battery, until I found the one swimsuit I owned. It was a questionable shade of black that had mostly faded to gray, at this point I supposed I just had to hope it didn't disintegrate the second I stepped into a pre-sauna shower.

Oh god, I was going to be showering. With Fletcher. Getting sweaty in a hot sauna, *with Fletcher*. It was hard to forget someone when they kept popping up uninvited into your life. No, it was going to be fine. Fletcher didn't want to be around me anymore than I wanted to be around him, we would find an amicable way to avoid each other, take turns in the sauna and have a great (or at least not terrible) trip with minimal interaction.

How worried did I really need to be? Should I be treating this like seeing an ex for the first time? I glanced into the large mirror hanging in my hallway as I made my way towards the front door. My green eyes looked a little bigger than usual and spots of colour had flared to life at the tops of my cheekbones, this often happened when I thought about Fletcher and our night together. Which wasn't frequently, damn it.

I raised my arms and gave my pits a quick sniff, rummaged in my bag and slicked on a little extra deodorant for the inevitable nervous sweats I was going to have. Being trapped in a car with a man who was so ashamed of our night together that he'd left before I'd woken up was not going to be good for my nerves *or* my self-esteem.

I pressed my hand to my face and breathed into it just as the doorbell rang and I whipped it away so fast I almost caught myself across the cheek. He was here. Would he look the same? Maybe he wasn't as gorgeous as I remembered, all long-lashes, golden skin and floppy blonde-brown hair that I'd run my hands through while we–

No. I wasn't going there. I needed to open the door, smile and say hello, and then sit in silence for the three hours it would take to get to the cabin in the middle of nowhere that Rob and Tanya had booked.

I hadn't even had the chance to do my last minute packing checks, too distracted by anxiety and last-minute swimsuit rummaging. Well, if I hadn't already packed it the likelihood was that it was something I could live without for a week or so.

There was a blurry silhouette showing through the frosted glass of my front door and my body trembled all over. *Don't be ridiculous,* I thought to myself, *he's just a man.*

I flung the door open and Fletcher jumped. Maybe he was just as nervous as I was trying not to be.

His cheeks were flushed from the cold and his lips parted as he took me in and well, *fuck.* He looked just as good as I remembered. He had on blue jeans, boots and a thick knit sweater and scarf. His hair looked soft, free of the gel he'd worn at Rob's wedding, and the lines by his eyes crinkled when he gave me a strained smile.

"Hi," I said and Fletcher's smile instantly dropped like just the sound of my voice was enough to offend him.

"Hey," he said evenly, voice empty of any emotion and the small flame of heat still burning inside me tried to gutter out, but the tightly balled fists at his side gave some idiotic part of me hope. For what, I had no clue. *He's an asshole,* I reminded myself, *don't forget about the note.* I held on to that thought, trying to keep it at the forefront of my mind as my eyes travelled over his broad shoulders and the planes of his chest, visible even through the chunky sweater. "Are you ready?" he asked, a small bite of impatience in his voice and I nodded, lifting my duffel and moving to step out of the house but found myself blocked by a well-muscled arm. I breathed through my mouth, trying to keep the scent of his cologne out of my nose and my head as I looked up at him with raised brows.

"I think you're forgetting something," Fletcher said, a small smirk twitching over his lips and vanishing as quickly as it came. *Hell yes,* I thought, I was trying to forget a whole damn lot – namely, *him.* He nodded behind me and I turned to look at what he was pointing at, my face burning a thousand shades of red as I saw my bikini bottoms lying on the floor by the shoe rack, apparently having fallen from my hand before I could shove them in my bag.

"Thanks," I muttered as I bent to scoop them up and stow them away. There was something odd in Fletcher's eyes as I moved back to him, something that took me back to *that* night once more. I focused on my breathing, gesturing Fletcher to move out of the way as I stepped out of the house, locked the door and strode over to the shiny black SUV in my driveway.

Don't be stupid. He didn't want me. He'd made that

abundantly clear when I'd woken up at 11AM to cold sheets and a hastily scrawled note half crumpled on his pillow. *This never happened.*

Damn right it hadn't and I was going to do my best to pretend exactly that.

CPSIA information can be obtained
at www.ICGtesting.com
Printed in the USA
LVHW032031040223
738684LV00007B/528

9 781739 145774